Strange stories of

Robert Shackleton et al.

Alpha Editions

This edition published in 2024

ISBN : 9789362994288

Design and Setting By
Alpha Editions
www.alphaedis.com
Email - info@alphaedis.com

Contents

INTRODUCTION

TO the younger readers of the twentieth century the great war of 1861-65, fought to maintain the authority of the national government and to preserve the union of the States, may sometimes seem remote and impersonal. The passage of time has healed the bitterness and animosity which an older generation can remember, and if proof were needed of the real union of our country it was shown when South and North marched side by side under the old flag in the war with Spain. It is well that the passions of war should be laid aside, but the examples of heroism on both sides and the lessons of patriotism are something always to be kept in mind. Grant and Lee, Sherman, Sheridan, "Stonewall" Jackson—figures like these arenot to be forgotten—and personal views of some of these leaders will be found in this book.

Of the great campaigns of those terrible four years, when vast armies marched and countermarched and wrestled in battles of giants, there are many accounts, and yet the necessarily limited space allotted in short histories may well be supplemented by narratives alive with human interest. That is the purpose of this book. Mr. Henderson's recollections, which serve as a prologue, will take the boy of to-day back to these eventful years and make him realize what it was to live in the days when North and South were summoning their sons to arms. Mr. Shackleton's dramatic story is the first of some imaginative tales of the war which aim to preserve the atmosphere of those thrilling days in the guise of fiction. The stories which follow—"The Blockade Runner" and "Two Days with Mosby," are believed to be essentially relations of actual experiences; and the balance of the book, including the tales of Lincoln, Worden and the Monitor, Sheridan'sRide, and Lee's surrender, is vivid, first-hand history. One feature of this book is that the latter stories are told by those who took an actual part. This is a book of adventure and of heroic deeds, which are not only of absorbing interest, but they also bring a closer realization of the one country which was welded together in the furnace of the Civil War.

More extended versions of the narratives by L. E. Chittenden and General G. A. Forsyth are presented in the former's Recollections of Lincoln and the latter's Thrilling Days of Army Life.

I
A BOY'S IMPRESSIONS OF THE CIVIL WAR

EVERY time I see the citizen soldiers of the National Guard march down the avenue I have a choking sensation in my throat, and sometimes tears come to my eyes. A young man who stood beside me one day when I could not help making an exhibition of myself, said, "What's the matter with you?" And my answer was, "They make me think of the men I saw going to the front in war-times." Then the young man laughed, and said, "What can you remember of the war?" He was about twenty-three or twenty-four years of age, and the Civil War was to him something to be read of in a dusty book. I was five years old when the war began. I could read and write, and was going to school. Many of the things which I saw then made impressions on my mind never to be effaced this side of the grave.

I was living in the city of Pittsburg, at the junction of the Alleghany and Monongahela rivers, whose waters, joined in the Ohio, flowed past many a field that will live in history. Pittsburg was not in the midst of the war, but it was close enough to some scenes of action, especially Gettysburg, and important enough as a point of departure and source of supplies to keep it filled with soldiers, and warmly in touch with all that was going on. What I wish to tell you is something about the way it all appeared to a boy.

My first recollection is of my father reading from a newspaper the announcement that Major Anderson and his garrison at Fort Sumter had been fired upon. That was in April, 1861, and I was in my sixth year; but I remember that I was greatly excited, and wondered what it all meant. It must have been later than that when my father gave me an explanation, which I remember to this day. He said: "My little boy, there is war between the people of the North and those of the South. The people in the South want to have slaves, and the people in the North say they must not have them. So the people of the South say they will not belong to the United States any more, and the people of the North say they must. And so they are fighting, and the fighting will go on till one or the other is beaten."[1]

All at once Pittsburg became alive with military preparations. Drums were beating in the streets all day and far into the night. Every hour a detachment of soldiers would march along Smithfield Street, and as I lived just above the corner of it on Second Street, now called Second Avenue, I would run to see every squad go by, till it became tiresome, and nothing short of a regiment could interrupt my play. Those must have been the seventy-five thousand volunteers called for by Abraham Lincoln to serve three months and crush the rebellion. Some of those men came back at the end of their three months, but of that I remember little or nothing. The only thing that made a strong impression on me in the early days of the war, after the attack on Sumter, was the killing of Ellsworth. I suppose every boy knows now how the gallant young Colonel of the New York Fire Zouaves took down the Confederate flag that was flying over an inn in Alexandria, and was shot dead by the proprietor of the house, who was immediately killed by Private Brownell.

That incident fired the hearts of all the boys in Pittsburg. We could not understand much of what we heard about the movements of troops, and I have forgotten everything which may have reached my ears at the time. But we could understand the murder of Ellsworth, and to this day I remember how we little fellows burned with indignation, and how we all wished we had been Brownell to shoot down the innkeeper. Somehow the untimely fate of the brave young Zouave commander appealed to us very forcibly, and I think some of us cried about it. It appealed to our mothers too, and suddenly the little boys in Pittsburg began to blossom out in Zouave suits. My mother had one made for me—a light-blue jacket with brass buttons, a red cap, and red trousers. She bought me a little flag, and had my picture taken in my uniform, and she has that picture yet. Next she got me a little tin sword; and then two older boys procured blue army overcoats and caps, and borrowed two muskets from the property-man at the theatre, and I used to drill those boys, and march them proudly all over Pittsburg, to the intense delight of the grown-up people, who cheered us wherever we went.

The next thing which remains indelibly fixed in my memory is the surprise and terror which flashed across the whole North when we heard the news from Bull Run. Of course I do not remember the date of the battle, and I am obliged to refer to my history to find that it took place in July, 1861. But we boys in Pittsburg had been indulging in much loud talk, as boys will, of the way in which our soldiers were going to blow out the rebellion, as one would blow out a candle; and here came the news that these miserable rebels, whom we despised, had thrashed our glorious army terribly, and were thinking about walking into Washington. My impressions at the time were that a lot of Southern slave-drivers, armed with snake whips and wearing slouch-hats, would soon arrive in Pittsburg and make us all stand around and obey orders. My father about this time used to pace the floor in deep thought after reading the newspaper, and used to set off for business with a bowed head. Later in life I learned that in those days he drew his last twenty-five dollars out of the bank, and did not know where more was to come from. But I thought he expected to be killed or made a slave. The boys used to discuss what steps they would take if the rebels came, and it was pretty generally agreed that we would all have to run across the Monongahela River bridge, climb Coal Hill, and hide in the mines.

From the time of Bull Run to the assassination of Abraham Lincoln my boyhood memories, as they come back to me now, present no orderly sequence of events. In a dim way I remember the distress and consternation caused by the dread event at Ball's Bluff, and in an equally uncertain way I remember how we cheered and danced when the news of a victory arrived. Just across the street from my father's house stood the Homœopathic Hospital, and next to it was a vacant lot in which pig-iron was stored. There we boys were wont to resort. We sat on the piles of pig metal and gravely discussed the progress of the war, and I well remember that one of my earliest combats arose from my proclaiming my belief that General Burnside was a greater man than George B. McClellan. That was rank treason; but I think Burnside's whiskers made a conquest of me. I will add that the dispute ended in a triumphant victory for the defender of McClellan's fame. Thereupon I went home to my mother and "told on" the defender. I got little consolation, for my mother said: "Don't come to me. If a boy hits you, you must hit back; but don't come in crying to me." We were a warlike race in those days.

Gettysburg is a word that conjures up memories for me. We thought we had seen soldiers in Pittsburg before that, but we had simply seen samples. When the Confederates invaded Pennsylvania, we found ourselves in a most unpleasant place; but we had plenty of excitement. From early dawn till late at night drums were beating in the streets and the walls of the houses echoed the tread of many feet. For three weeks I never set my foot inside the Second Ward School in Ross Street, where I was supposed to be, but every morning I stole quietly across the bridge and ascended Coal Hill. Do you know what was going on up there? Soldiers were working like beavers, throwing up earthworks. Similar operations were in progress on every hill around the city, and many an hour I spent carrying water for the boys in the hot sun.

When I descended the hill I always went to the yard at the Birmingham end of the bridge, and watched the workmen who were building Monitors. I do not remember how many Monitors were built there, but I remember very distinctly seeing the launch of the Manayunk. Later she steamed away down the Ohio, and I knew no more of her. The original Monitor, the wonderful little craft that so ably defended the Minnesota in Hampton Roads, was my special object of worship in those days. Little did I dream then that I should live to know the sea as well as I do, or to drill on the deck of the Minnesota. The Monitor's success in her great duel with the Merrimac filled all of us boys with excitement. We promptly built Monitors with round boxes placed on shingles sharpened at both ends. Then we made

Merrimacs of an equally rude type. Next we went down to the river, and in the still water between the big stern-wheelers that lay with their noses against the levee, we had some of the most tremendous naval engagements that ever escaped the eye of history. And the Merrimac was always defeated, whereupon she retreated up the river and promptly blew herself up. Those were good times!

But when the man came with the Great Diorama of the War we learned something new. A diorama is, to be Hibernian, just like a panorama, only it is different. In a panorama you see pictures; in a diorama you see moving figures cut out in profile. After each scene the curtain must be lowered and the stage reset. I remember that this man (I wish I knew his name) began his entertainment with an ordinary series of panoramic views, after which the curtain fell, and we prepared ourselves for the new revelation. When the curtain rose again, we saw a miniature stage set with scenic waters. In the background were two large ships, cut out in profile, and in the distance were two or three more. The next moment we were startled by seeing a flash shoot out from the side of one, followed by a dull boom. Then the other big ship fired, and next the forts, which were at the sides, opened up. We began to tingle with excitement, and could hardly remain in our seats.

Suddenly a long, low craft, looking something like an inverted cake-pan, came gliding out at the front of the stage. Then we knew we were looking at the feared and hated Merrimac. She opened fire on the ships. Then she circled round, and, putting on steam, rushed against one of them with her ram. The poor wooden vessel careened far over on one side. Then the Merrimac drew back, and hurled two shots into her at short range. The big ship began to sink. She went clear away down out of sight—royals, trucks, and all. Next the Merrimac went for the other ship; but just then we saw another queer craft sail on. "It was the immortal cheese-box on a plank"— the Monitor. The Merrimac paused. The two iron-clads seemed to stop and look at each other. Then they rushed together. And how they spit fire and banged and butted! We boys were crazy with excitement. And when suddenly the Merrimac blew up with a loud report, and the Monitor displayed half a dozen American flags, we cheered till we were hoarse. It was not strictly according to history, but it was glorious. And we boys went right home, and began building a Grand Diorama of the War in the cellar of the St. Charles Hotel the next day. That diorama would have been a tremendous success but for one thing. Jim Rial's brother dropped a match into the powder-bottle, which blew up the diorama and nearly blinded the boy. However, we built another diorama; and the boy got well.

But to return to Gettysburg. When troops were being hurried forward to that point from every direction, thousands of soldiers passed through Pittsburg. Many of them were sent out by the Pittsburg and Connellsville

Railroad to Uniontown, and thence to the front. Every afternoon I used to go to the Connellsville station, at the foot of Ross Street, and ride out on the four-o'clock train as far as the historic Braddock's Field, where, you remember, the British commander Braddock refused to take Washington's advice in the matter of Indian-fighting, and paid the penalty. This station was just ten miles out, and I could get back in time for supper. Attached to every train out in those days were several flat-cars with planks laid across from side to side for seats, and these cars were loaded with soldiers. I always rode in one of those cars, and listened in breathless awe to the conversation of those real live soldiers who were going out to fight. As I remember them now, they were hearty, good-natured fellows, very kind to the little boy who took so much interest in them. And when I returned to Pittsburg I used to dream about them at night, and wake up very early in the morning to listen for the sound of the guns of the approaching invaders. I was no worse than older people. Many a good woman in Pittsburg went on the roof very often to listen for those same guns.

Another thing which I remember very distinctly is the work we used to do in the public schools in those days. Every afternoon we devoted a part of our time to picking lint. We were told by our teachers that it was to be sent to the front, where it would be used in dressing the wounds of the soldiers. None of us dreamed of the real horrors of war, but I think our hearts were in that work just the same. And we used to get our mothers to make housewives, which we filled with combs, brushes, and soap; and these, too, were sent to the front. We saw soldiers going to war every day with no other baggage than their knapsacks, and we well understood, children as we were, that the housewife would be welcome in every tent.

And finally came the news of Appomattox. Guns were fired, and people cheered, and we boys simply danced war-dances all over the city. Soon the troops began to come home, and then we had our eyes opened a bit. The boys of to-day see the old fellows of the Grand Army of the Republic turn out in their sober blue uniforms, carrying the old battle-flags carefully wrapped up, and the boys think them a monotonous lot, and take little interest in them. But I saw them come back with their bare feet sticking out of their ragged shoes, with the legs of their trousers and the arms of their coats hanging in tatters, with the army blue faded by the sun and washed by the rain to a sickly greenish-gray, with their faces baked and frozen and blown till they looked like sheets of sole-leather, saving the happy smiles they bore. And I saw those old battle-flags come back with their rent and shivered stripes streaming in the wind, while strong men stood looking on with tears in their eyes. And I saw one of my uncles, who had been a prisoner in Andersonville, come to Pittsburg with a gangrened foot, which my mother dressed every day. I shall never forget his condition, nor that of the heroes who marched through Pittsburg day after day when the war was over. I am sorry there had to be a war; but I am unspeakably grateful that I was old enough to get those impressions, which will live as long as I do. They spring to life again whenever I see troops on the march, and they give the old flag a meaning for me which I think it cannot have for those without my memories.

II
THE CAPTAIN OF COMPANY Q

The Tale of an Unenlisted Soldier

ZEBEDEE was the Captain of Company Q. Sheer merit had won him the title. He was the first and the last of his kind. He stood unique. For it was the only Company Q that had ever been captained—Company Q being the stragglers and camp-followers, miscellaneous and heterogeneous, who drift in an army's wake.

Unique though Zebedee's position was, it was far from satisfying the ambition that he had once cherished. For he had longed to be a soldier. He had dreamed of doing great deeds; of rising from the ranks, of steadily mounting upward, of winning lofty title and mighty fame.

But the surgeon curtly refused him. It was the heart, he said. And when Zebedee, amazed, bewildered, for he had never suspected himself to be a sick man, stammered a protest, the surgeon said a few cutting words about worthless men trying to get in for pay and pension—which words were to Zebedee as blows. And he yielded with such bleak finality as never again to ask for enlistment.

But although he himself could scarcely explain how it came to pass, he found himself a camp-follower, a drudge, a volunteer servant to the command of a general to whose fame he gave humble and admiring awe. At first the soldiers had tolerated him; gradually there had come a recognition of his willingness, his good-nature, his real cleverness. It somehow came to be believed that it was by some vagrant choice of his own that he was a member of Company Q, and none ever dreamed that he longed with pathetic intensity for his lost chance of being a soldier. On the march he wore a look of exaltation whenever, which was not seldom, two or three of the men would carelessly give him their muskets to carry. In the camp he was happy if he could do some service—he would chop wood, build fires, and cook. And in time of battle he was perforce resigned when the soldiers marched by him into the smoke and the roar, leaving him behind to hold some officer's horse or look after some tent.

But the innate spirit that, if given the opportunity, would have carried him far upward, made him master of the motley members of Q, and it gradually came to be that his words had the force of law with them.

He never assumed a complete uniform. His very reverence for it and for all that it represented kept him from such a height of undeserved glory. But he tried to satisfy his craving soul with the tattered jacket of an artilleryman, a shabby cavalry cap, and the breeches of infantry; and the sartorial dissimilitude, through the working of some obscure logic, obviated presumption yet kept alive some pride.

How it happened that Zebedee was so often in dangerous places which the other members of Company Q carefully avoided was a puzzle to the soldiers, and it came to be ascribed to a sort of blundering heedlessness—not bravery, of course, for he was only a camp-follower.

And one day, when the command failed in its attack upon a fort, Zebedee found himself with the handful who fled for safety close up against the hostile works. There they were protected from shots from above; and the enemy dared not, on account of a covering fire, come out into the open to attack them; and there they hoped to stay till darkness should permit retreat.

But the day was blisteringly hot, and thirst began to madden them. Then Zebedee slung about him a score of canteens, and dashed out across the plain, and lead rained pitilessly about him as he jingled on, but he was not hit. His canteens were swiftly filled by friendly hands, and he turned to go back across that deadly space.

THEN ZEBEDEE DASHED OUT ACROSS THE PLAIN

He knew that fire would flash along the hostile works; that lead again would rain; but he did not waver. He saw the dark line of his comrades, he knew their misery, he could at least give one life for his country—and the men watched him with awe as, with a curious gravity, he, about to die, saluted them in farewell and ran unhesitatingly out. A sort of glory was upon his countenance. There was a hush. Friend and enemy alike were awed and still. No sound was heard but the rapid patter of his feet. There came no flash and smoke, no splintering sound of musketry. But there arose a mighty shout—friends and enemies alike were cheering him!—and he sank, hysterically sobbing, among his comrades.

This, of course, brought about important recognition. The General heard of it; heard, too, that the Captain of Company Q did not, from some crotchet, some whimsy, wish to be a regular soldier.

"Zebedee," he said, "you are a brave man."

Zebedee's heart beat high with hope, and the look of exaltation shone in his eyes. Not knowing whether or not to use words, or what words to use, he could only stand stiffly at salute—he knew how to salute, although no drill-master had ever paid attention to him; he had eagerly watched and practised, and was perfect at this as at many other things. He stood rigidly at salute—but his eyes were like the eyes of a faithful dog that hungrily watches his master for a bone.

"I am sorry you are not an enlisted man, Zebedee."

Ah! how high his heart beat now! To be a corporal—perhaps even a sergeant—

The General went on, speaking slowly so that the full sense of his condescension should sink in: "And so, you shall be my own personal servant."

Zebedee stood rigid as if he were a piece of mechanism, and all expression was swept from his face as marks are swept from a slate.

And having thus conferred honor, the General went out; he, the great warrior so able to discern the hidden movements of an opposing army, to read the secret plans of an enemy, but quite unable to discern the poignant suffering of a brave man.

Zebedee was a sturdy man, not given to running away or to changeableness. In his heart—the heart of which the surgeon had spoken so contemptuously—he had enlisted for the war; he would not be permitted, so it seemed, to fight the good fight, but he must patiently finish the course and keep the faith.

What mattered it now that by observation he had learned many things besides how to salute! With bitter resignation he would watch the coming and going of officers, the forms and ceremonies of war. At dress parade he knew just when the drums were to march slowly down from the right flank; just when there was to be the thrice-repeated, long, brisk roll; just when the drums were to turn back, with quicker step; just how the commanding officer out there in front would keep his hand upon the hilt of his sword; just when the adjutant would take his place at the front of the line; just when was to come the command, "First sergeants to the front and centre!" The roll of drums, and the crash of music, and the tramp of many feet— and the Captain of Company Q would turn away, his eyes filled with tears, as vague visions came of the heights to which he had aspired when he hurried to enlist—before he knew he had a heart. But he knew it now; he knew it, and it hurt.

In the uncommunicative companionship of General and servant he learned much. He learned to know and almost to love the stern, strong man, who held his men in iron discipline and led them into battle with a fierceness that was almost joy.

There came, too, a sort of liking for Zebedee on the part of the grim officer. He trusted him, sometimes let him write orders, treated him with a curt kindliness, and often permitted him to remain within hearing when discussions went on.

And Zebedee, still in touch with Company Q, which stood more in awe of him than ever, and in touch, since his day of glory, with the men, came also to know and to understand the officers. By observation, divination, putting together this and that, he came to know how much depended upon the personality of the General, and how bitter was the rivalry among those next in command; he knew that they would do their utmost under the overmastering influence of their leader's spirit, but that jealousy and laxity would work disaster should the potent headship be lost.

And with this there came to Zebedee a new sense of responsibility and pride. When so much depended upon the General, surely the importance was great of the servant who saw to it that he should sleep in comfort and properly eat!

He no longer wore the old clothes whose acquisition had been such pride to him. The General had given him some of his own cast-off things, which fitted him measurably well and relieved the shabbiness of effect which would not have consorted with his present dignity.

There had been a day of fighting, a day of doubt. The General, almost overwhelmingly outnumbered, had fought with splendid skill. But as night fell there went shiveringly through the ranks the rumor that he had been desperately hurt.

The General lay unconscious in his tent. Absolute quiet had been ordered. Zebedee must watch him, nurse him, tend him, and the sentinels must keep even the highest officers away. The sentinels' duty would be well done, for iron discipline had taught each man to hold the General's tent a thing sacred.

Absolute silence had been ordered. And, as if heeding, the rattle of musketry died away, the sullen cannon stopped from muttering, even there ceased the sound of trampling feet, of rolling wagons, of the swinging tinkle of canteens. Only the chirring hum of frogs and katydids and tree-toads, the multitudinous murmur of a Virginia summer night, was heard. Then from far in the distance came solemnly the strain, "My country, 'tis of thee," and the soul of Zebedee was thrilled and uplifted as never before in his poor life.

Once in a while the chief surgeon hurried back from the multitude of other cases that the day had given. In piercing anxiety Zebedee watched by the General's side. "Has there been any change?" "There has been no change."

Slowly the hours marched towards morning. The chief surgeon again appeared and led Zebedee outside the tent. "There will be an advance and an engagement at daybreak. The General will sleep for hours. I may be unable to come in again for a while. Be sure to let him sleep. I depend upon you, Zebedee."

Zebedee had held all surgeons to be his enemies, but here was one that roused his humble devotion. And the words crystallized a feeling which had already come over him with almost oppressive weight—the feeling that upon him, Zebedee, there lay a heavy responsibility. He thought of the renewed battle, now so imminent, and as by a flash of inspiration he saw the results of jealousy and half-hearted co-operation; he saw the soldiers, like frightened children, making an ineffectual stand; the impotency of his position came upon him like pain.

He glanced from the tent. A nebulous lustre marked the glow from the enemy's fires. Through the air came faintly the mysterious light that tells of the coming of morning. A dull slow wind crept laggard by. Statued sentinels stood stiff and still. Two dimly outlined aides conversed in cautious sibilation. Silently he drew back and returned to the General's side.

The General still slept. To Zebedee's anxious ears a soft thudding told of soldiers marching through the feeble light. The sound increased. He knew that shadows were passing by. There was the crunch of heavy wheels and he knew that cannon, sulkily tossing their lowered heads from side to side, were being dragged unwillingly towards fight. Faintly audible firing began in the far distance, and the sulky cannon set up a hoarse and excited cry.

The laggard dawn came with a plumping rain. The candle in the bayonet end flamed yellow. The sounds of distant battle grew more loud.

The General opened his eyes. He sighed with a great weariness. He listened to the sounds, and thought himself again a boy, on a farm, hearing the homely noise of breakfast-dishes and milk-cans and wagons. "I can't get up—I'm tired," he said, and his voice was as the querulous voice of a boy. His eyes fell upon Zebedee, and the tense look of dread anxiety almost roused him. He sat up; then fell back, smiling quietly. "I have always trusted you, Zebedee," he said, simply, in such a tone as Zebedee had never before heard; "always—trusted—you." And with that, he was dead.

Dead, and the battle was on. To Zebedee it meant the end of all things precious. His mind in its agony lost all sense of proportion. The General was dead!—that was the one important fact in all the universe.

A shell flew over the tent. Already the enemy were advancing! Another shell, and another and another. They fascinated him. In their sounds they marked the full range of life and of passion. One shrieked, one groaned, one muttered like a miser counting gold, one whispered like a child, one was petulant, one expostulated, one whispered softly like a maid confessing love. Zebedee shivered. Suddenly the shell sounds turned to taunts. He could have wept from very impotence. He felt choking, smothered. Passionate cannon began a louder uproar.

The General was dead. Yes; that was the one important fact in all the universe. He, only he, knew!—And suddenly there came an awesome thought.

Even from the first frightened contemplation of it he snatched a fearful joy. He steadied himself. He drew himself up to his full height. He drew a deep breath and stretched out his arms as a man preparing for some feat of strength. His face grew strange, and a thousand tiny wrinkles aged him as the thought bewilderingly grew. His breath came in queer respirations.

The sinister droning of another shell—and doubt fell from him like a garment.

The astonished aides saw the General come forth into the rain, with hat drawn over his face and collar turned up high. Something of menacing austerity in his motions repressed all words of sympathy or dissuasion. In an instant he was upon a horse and had set off at headlong gallop for the front.

Panic had already begun. Men were confusedly huddling, firing distractedly and at random. A curious quaking cry was beginning to arise—the cry of frightened men in hysteria; and ranks were beginning to crumble, and soldiers were on the verge of tumultuous retreat.

But now the General was there! Like magic the news spread. His very presence checked the panic and hysteria. He gave a few quick orders, in a voice so tense and strange that the officers scarcely knew it. His wild, stark energy stirred officers and men into invincibleness. It was as if the fate of all the world and all time hung upon what he could accomplish in the few minutes thus permitted him. He dared not stop to think.

Slowly the enemy crumbled. The sun struggled through the clouds and the colors shone in glorified indistinctness in a wet glitter of sunlight.

It was over now. He turned his horse and rode slowly back towards the tent. "Don't follow me," he said, curtly. And he rode back, slowly and alone. The cry of the cannon was now triumphant and glad. A shell, whirling above him, spluttered in futile animosity. The wild cheering was music to his ears.

His dream was over now—the dream he had dreamed when he longed to enlist. He flung up his arms and laughed aloud. His dream! To enlist as a private, to win patiently through grades of sergeant and lieutenant, to captain and colonel and general in command!

He wearily dropped from his horse. He went into the tent. The Captain of Company Q looked down upon the General's peaceful face.

———————————————————

III
MIDSHIPMAN JACK, U.S.N.

The Action of Appalachicola

"I AM not one of those fellows who 'can fight and run away, and live to fight some other day,'" one of the bravest Lieutenant-Commanders in the United States navy said one evening to a party of friends, who were making him feel uncomfortable by discussing his brilliant war record. "My bad leg won't let me run, so I always have to stand and fight it out."

"Why, Commander," one of his friends exclaimed, "I did not know that you had a bad leg. You do not limp."

"No," he answered, "not ordinarily. But when I tire myself I limp a little, and if I were to undertake to run I should come to grief."

"Where did you receive your injury?" another asked.

"In action at Appalachicola," the Commander replied; "the severest action I ever saw."

There was a twinkle in his eyes as he spoke, and he looked about the table to see what effect the words had upon his friends. Two of them merely muttered their sympathy, and the third asked for the story of the fight; but the fourth man looked up with a comical expression that told the Commander he was understood in one quarter at least.

"You will certainly have to tell us about that," this fourth man laughed, seeing that the Commander was waiting for a question; "for I have always understood that Appalachicola, being an out-of-the-way place, was one of the few Southern towns that escaped without a scratch in the war. I never heard of any battle there."

"No, there was no battle there," the Commander replied, "and you would hardly hear of the action, because there were so few engaged in it. In fact, I was the only one on the Federal side, and there were no Confederates. When I was a boy there I fell out of a pine-tree and broke my thigh; so it was my own action, and one that I still have reason to remember."

This was the Commander's modest way of describing an accident that brought out all the manliness he had in him, and made him an officer in the United States navy, and he seldom gives any other account of it; but some of the grown-up boys of Appalachicola tell the story in a very different way—the same "boys," some of them, who used to set out in parties of three or four and chase young Jack Radway and make life miserable for him.

Jack had a strange habit, when he was between fifteen and sixteen (this is the way they tell the story in Appalachicola), of going down to the wharf and sitting by the half-hour on the end of a spile, looking out over the bay. That was in 1862. His name was not Jack Radway, but that is a fairly good sort of name, and on account of the Commander's modesty it will have to answer for the present. While he sat in this way it was necessary for him to keep the corner of one eye on the wharf and the adjacent street, watching for enemies. Oddly enough, every white boy in the town was Jack's enemy, generous as he was, and brave and good-hearted; and when one came alone, or even two, if they were not too big, he was always ready to stay and defend himself. But when three or four came together he was forced to retire to his father's big brick warehouse, across the street. They would not follow him there, because it was well known that the rifle standing beside the desk was always kept loaded.

This enmity with the other boys, for no fault of his own, was Jack's great sorrow. A year or two before he had been a favorite with all the boys and girls, and now he was hungry for a single friend of his own age. The reason of it was that his father was the only Union man in Appalachicola. Every white man, woman, and child in the town sympathized with the Confederacy, except John Radway and his wife and their son Jack. The elder Radway had thought it over when the trouble began, and had made up his mind that his allegiance belonged to the old government that his grandfather had fought for.

Near the mouth of the river lay the United States gun-boat Alleghany, guarding the harbor, with the stars and stripes floating bravely at her stern.

"Look at that flag," Jack's father told him. "Your great-grandfather fought for it, and I want you always to honor it. It is the grandest flag in the whole world. It is my flag and yours, and you must never desert it."

By the side of Mr. Radway's house stood a tall pine-tree, much higher than the top of the house, with no limbs growing out of the trunk except at the very top, after the manner of Southern pines. Jack was a great climber, and nearly every day, when he did not go down-town, he "shinned" up this tall tree to make sure that the gun-boat was still in the harbor. And one day, the day of what the Commander calls "the action at Appalachicola," he lost his hold in some way, or a limb broke, and he fell from the top to the ground.

For some time he lay there unconscious, and when he came to his senses he could not get up. There was a terrible pain in his left hip, and he called for help, and his mother and some of the colored women ran out and carried him into the house, and when they laid him on a bed he fainted again from the pain.

Mr. Radway was sent for, and after he had examined the leg as well as he could, he looked very solemn, for there was no doubt that the bone was badly broken. Even Jack, young as he was, could tell that; but with all his pain he made no complaint.

"This is serious business," Mr. Radway said to his wife when they were out of Jack's hearing. "The bone is badly fractured at the thigh, and there is not a doctor left in Appalachicola to set it. Every one of them is away in the army, and I don't know of a doctor within a hundred miles."

"Except on the gun-boat," Mrs. Radway interrupted; "there must be a surgeon on the gun-boat."

"I have thought of that," Mr. Radway answered; "but if he should come ashore he would almost certainly be killed, so I could not ask him to come. And if I should take Jack out to the boat, we would very likely be attacked on the way. I must take time to think."

Medicines were scarce in Appalachicola in those days, but they gave Jack a few drops of laudanum to ease the pain, and made a cushion of pillows for his leg. For all his terrible suffering, and the doubt about getting the bone set, he did not utter a word of complaint. But he turned white as the pillows, and the great heat of midsummer on the shore of the Gulf added to his misery.

For hours Mr. Radway walked the floor, trying to make up his mind what to do. Jack's suffering was agony to him, and the uncertainty of getting help increased it. Late in the evening, when all the household were in bed but Mr. and Mrs. Radway, they heard the sound of many feet coming up the walk, then a shuffling of feet on the piazza, and a heavy knock at the front door.

"Have they the heart for that?" Mr. Radway exclaimed. "Could they come to attack us when they know what trouble we are in? Some of them shall pay dearly for it if they have."

The knock was repeated, louder than before, and Mr. Radway took up a rifle and started for the door. Standing the rifle in the corner of the wall, and with a cocked revolver in one hand, he turned the key and opened the door a crack, keeping one foot well braced against it.

"You don't need your gun, neighbor," said the spokesman of the party without; "it's a peaceable errand we are on this time."

"What is it?" Mr. Radway asked, still suspicious.

"COULD THEY COME TO ATTACK US WHEN THEY KNOW WHAT TROUBLE WE ARE IN?"

"We know the trouble you are in," the man continued, "and we are sorry for you. It's not John Radway we are down on; it's his principles; but we want to forget them till we get you out of this scrape. There are twenty of us here, all your neighbors and former friends. We know there is no doctor in Appalachicola, and we have come to say that if you can get the surgeon of the gun-boat to come ashore and mend up the sick lad, he shall have safe-conduct both ways. We will guard him ourselves, and we pledge our word that not a hair of his head shall be touched."

This friendly act came nearer to breaking down John Radway's bold front than all the persecutions he had been subjected to. He threw the door wide open, put the revolver in his pocket, and grasped the spokesman's hand.

"I need not try to thank you," he said; "you know what I would say if I could. My poor Jack is in great pain, and I shall make up my mind between this and daylight what had better be done."

The knowledge that he was surrounded by friends instead of enemies made Jack feel better in a few minutes; but the pain was too great to be relieved permanently in such a way, and all night long he lay with his teeth shut tight, determined to make no complaint.

By daylight he was in such a high fever that his father had no further doubts about what to do. He must have medical attendance at once; and the quickest way was to take him out to the gun-boat, rather than risk the delay of getting the surgeon ashore. So a cot-bed was converted into a stretcher by lashing handles to the sides. Colored men were sent for to carry it, and another was sent down to the shore to make Mr. Radway's little boat ready.

The morning sun was just beginning to gild the smooth water of Appalachicola Bay, when the after-watchman on the gun-boat's deck, who for some time had been watching a little sail-boat with half a table-cloth flying at the mast-head, called out:

"Small flag-of-truce boat on the port quarter!"

Jack Radway, lying on the stretcher in the bottom of the boat, heard the words repeated in a lower tone, evidently at the door of the Captain's cabin: "Small flag-of-truce boat on the port quarter, sir."

An instant later a young officer appeared at the rail with a marine-glass in his hand.

"Ahoy there in the boat!" he called. "Put up your helm! Sheer off!"

The Alleghany lay in an enemy's waters, and she was not to be caught napping. Nothing was allowed to approach without giving a good reason for it.

Then Jack's father stood up in the boat. "I have a boy here with a broken thigh," he said. "I want your surgeon to set it."

"Who are you?" the officer asked.

"John Radway—a loyal man," was the answer.

The name was as good as a passport, for the gun-boat people had heard of John Radway.

"Come alongside," the officer called; and five minutes later a big sailor had Jack in his arms, carrying him up the gangway, and he was taken into the boat's hospital and laid on another cot. It was an unusual thing on a naval vessel, and when the big bluff surgeon came the Captain was with him, and several more of the officers.

The examination gave Jack more pain than he had had before, but still he kept his teeth clinched, and refused even to moan.

"It is a bad fracture, and should have been attended to sooner," the surgeon said at length. "There is nothing to be done for it now but to take off the leg."

"Oh, I hope not!" Mr. Radway exclaimed. "Is there no other way?"

"He knows best, father," Jack said; "he will do the best he can for me."

"He is too weak now for an operation," the surgeon continued; "but you can leave him with me, and I think by to-morrow he will be able to stand it."

If Jack had made the least fuss at the prospect of having his leg cut off, or had let a single groan escape, there is hardly any doubt that he would be limping through life on one leg. But the brave way that he bore the pain and the doctor's verdict made him a powerful friend.

The Captain of a naval vessel cannot control his surgeon's treatment of a case; but the Captain's wishes naturally go a long way, even with the surgeon. So it was a great point for Jack when the Captain interceded for him.

"There's the making of an Admiral in that lad in the hospital," the Captain told the doctor later in the day. "I never saw a boy bear pain better. I wish you would save his leg if you possibly can."

"He'd be well much quicker to take it off," the surgeon retorted. "But I'll give him every chance I can. There is a bare possibility that I may be able to save it."

There was joy in the Radway family when it became known that there was a chance of saving Jack's leg; but all that Jack himself would say was, "Leave it all to the doctor; he will do what he can."

Three weeks afterwards Jack still lay in the Alleghany's hospital with two legs to his body, but one half hidden in splints and plaster. Mr. and Mrs. Radway visited him every day, and the broken bone was healing so nicely that the doctor thought that in three or four weeks more Jack might be able to hobble about the deck on crutches, when more trouble came. A new gun-boat steamed into the harbor to take the Alleghany's place, bringing orders for the Alleghany to go at once to the Brooklyn Navy-Yard. This was particularly unfortunate for Jack, for his broken bone was just in that state where the motion of taking him ashore would be likely to displace it. But that unwelcome order from Washington proved to be a long step towards making Jack one of our American naval heroes.

"It would be a great risk to take him ashore," the surgeon said to Mr. Radway. "The least movement of the leg would set him back to where we began. You had much better let him go North with us. The voyage will do him good; and even if we are not sent back here, he can easily make his way home when he is able to travel."

Nothing could have suited Jack better than this, for he had become attached to the gun-boat and her officers; so it was soon settled that he was to lie still on his bed and be carried to Brooklyn. For more than a month he lay there without seeing anything of the great city on either side of him; and the Alleghany was already under orders to sail for Key West before he was able to venture on deck with a crutch under each arm. There were delays in getting away, so by the time the gun-boat was steaming down the coast Jack was walking slowly about her deck with a cane, and the color was in his cheeks again and the old sparkle in his eyes. He was in hopes of finding a schooner at Key West that would carry him to Appalachicola; but he was not to see the old town again for many a day.

The Alleghany was a little below Hatteras, when she sighted a Confederate blockade-runner, and she immediately gave chase. But, much to the surprise of the officers, this blockade-runner did not run away, as they generally did. She was much larger than the Alleghany, and well manned and armed, and she preferred to stay and fight. Almost before he knew it Jack was in the midst of a hot naval battle. The two vessels were soon close together, and there was such a thunder of guns and such a smother of smoke that he does not pretend to remember exactly what happened. But after it was all over, and the blockade-runner was a prize, with the stars and stripes flying from her stern, Jack walked as straight as anybody down to the little hospital where he had spent so many weeks.

His mother would hardly have known him as he stepped into the hospital and waited till the surgeon had time to take a big splinter from his left arm.

"Where's your cane, young man?" the surgeon asked, when Jack's turn came.

"I don't know, sir!" Jack replied, surprised to find himself standing without it. "I must have forgotten all about it. I saw one of the gunners fall, and I took his place, and that's all I remember, sir, except seeing the enemy strike her colors."

That action made Jack a Midshipman in the United States navy, and gave him a share in the prize-money, and a year later he was an Ensign. For special gallantry in action in Mobile Bay he was made a Lieutenant before the close of the war, and in the long years since then he has risen more slowly to the rank of Lieutenant-Commander.

IV
CAPTAIN BILLY

Aid and Comfort to the Enemy

WHEN the General invited the Fortescue girls and their friends to spend an evening in the house on the Square, it was always understood that part of the entertainment was to be a "war story," and, on the special evening I refer to, a barrel of apples, sent from the "northern part of the State," gave the subject.

"Oh yes, Molly," said the General to the girl, whom the old nurse now called "the eldest Miss Fortescue," "you can put the apples out; and they've just made me remember I never told you about 'Tobacco Billy,'" and as his eager auditors settled themselves comfortably about the fire, the General, with his peculiar quiet smile, began.

"Just hand me down that old photograph in the little black frame; there you are—poor old Tobacco Billy!"

"Old!" exclaimed Tom Fortescue, in surprise, for the picture was that of a plain-looking, rather gawky lad of only nineteen—a "boy in blue"—with honesty and fearlessness in every line of his homely, gentle face.

"Well, I don't say in years, perhaps," said the General, "but in wisdom. Anyway, here's his story. Give that coal a stir, will you. Now, then, here we are:

"We were in camp, not very far from Charleston, and it was a pretty serious business with us. You see, we hadn't the least idea what the enemy were up to. My particular friend, Captain Kard, of the Confederate army, and I were talking about it not long ago, and he said he well remembered how, on their side, they were chuckling over our perplexity. Well, I must tell you that at the extreme end of our camp we had a bridge, and it was regularly patrolled by two of the men I picked out for the purpose, and the 'other side' had a place beyond similarly patrolled. If any message had to be sent over, the sentries reversed their guns as a signal of truce, and word was exchanged.

"Now although we were pretty badly off for provisions, and even ammunition, it wasn't a circumstance to the condition of the 'Johnnies,' as we called the gentlemen over the way, and, worst of all, the poor chaps hadn't the comfort of a 'smoke' even, which, as all soldiers will tell you, keeps the gnawing feeling of hunger away for a time at least. No, sir! they hadn't five pounds of tobacco in their camp. But never mind! I'll tell you what they did have. They had regularly every day a copy of their own Charleston paper, which, of course, was printed for Confederate eyes alone. I was sitting in my tent one night smoking and thinking and wondering how I could lay hands on one or two of those papers. You must know, my dear children, stratagem is always allowed and understood to be used on both sides in war. It is as much a part of the whole unhappy business as loading guns and firing them, and far better if it leads to peace and an end of cruel feeling. Now, if I could only get a copy or two of those papers, do you see, the key to the enemy's next movements might be in our hands, and I suddenly struck a bright idea. I sent a man to replace Billy Forbes on the bridge, and presently that lad appeared in my doorway. He saluted, and I motioned him to come inside. Then, after warning him of the need of secrecy and caution, I told him my dilemma. Billy rubbed his head, whistled softly, looked up and down anxiously, and finally, after a moment's star-gazing, 'Lieutenant,' says he, in his slow, Connecticut voice, 'I've hit on a way—if you don't mind.'

"'Go ahead, Billy,' I rejoined.

"'Well, sir, you see those poor devils have scarcely a chew or a smoke of 'baccy among them.'

"'How do you know?'

"'Johnny on the other side made signs, sir, and mate and I weren't slow to understand.'

"'Well. Go on.'

"'Now, if I could sneak over a bit from those great packages in the Quartermaster's department, and make him know what we were after, sure as guns, Lieutenant, you'd have the papers.'

"'Billy,' said I, 'you are a credit to your regiment, to say nothing of your Yankee mother. Come here in an hour, and I'll see you have the tobacco.'

"Some enterprising dealer in the North had received a contract for that lot of stuff, and we had really, for the time being, an overabundance, so that it was by no means a difficult matter for me to secure two half-pound packets, done up in blue paper, and in about as short a time as it takes to tell the story, Billy Forbes had it tucked away, and went whistling back to his post.

"It was a clear, soft, starlit night. I sat up attending to various duties—listening to the fussy complaints and talk of one of my colleagues in command, who had it on the brain, and felt we were disgraced not knowing how to get in there. Somehow, I relied on my friend Billy to win the day by his fair 'exchange,' and he didn't fail me.

"Towards morning I went down to the bridge, having sent a relief for the lad, who came back simply grinning.

"'Easy as could be,' he whispered. 'Here you are, sir.'

"And from the depths of his trousers he produced the coveted little sheets.

"'Billy,' said I, 'when the war is over you are likely to be a great man.'

"And I turned in to read the news.

"About ten o'clock I received an awful message, in answer to which I started post-haste for the guard-house, meeting my anxious comrade Captain Hubert on the way.

"'A nice mess your protégé is in, Lieutenant!' he exclaimed. 'I've had to put him under arrest, and he's doomed, sir, doomed. Will no doubt be shot, and a good warning to all like him.'

"As the Captain—in temporary command—marched on, I stood rooted to the ground. What had happened! Well, I soon found out. Billy, white to the lips, but with his head well up, told me the story. His companion, cherishing some old grudge, had watched him making the exchange—tobacco for the journals—and had made haste to report him. Billy well knew the penalty. A court-martial had to be held at once.

"Billy, poor lad, for violating the law which forbids absolutely giving aid or comfort to the enemy, must be shot! That was the law, and you must bear in mind that the well-being of a whole nation, especially in time of war, depends upon the strict discipline of the army being maintained. There were important reasons why I could not at that moment say I had, through Billy, procured the papers, and relieve him of the extreme penalty. Yet something must be done, and I must try and think it out, even though in discharging my duty I must sit in the court-martial which would undoubtedly condemn him.

"'Billy,' said I, with my hand on the lad's shoulder, and looking at his white and haggard young face, 'I'll do my best. Unless compelled to, don't mention the papers. That can't be known just yet.'

"'God bless you, sir,' said Billy, with tears rolling down his cheeks. 'You see, mother'd be proud if I had to die in battle; but shot down, Lieutenant, for treason—'

"Well, I can tell you, I couldn't stand it much longer, and I went dismally enough to the court-martial. You needn't imagine it was in any fine court-room. Dignified and often tragic as were the cases, the court sat in an old tool-shed; planks on barrels formed the tables, and for seats we had empty provision boxes turned upside down. But there was about it the solemnity of such an occasion—of a death charge, perhaps, and all the grave formality of the promptest law known. When in the paltry place the court-martial began I knew that my colleague, Captain Hubert, was in a great state of excitement, and determined, if possible, to 'put down' such recklessness as had been Billy Forbes's. We had some minor cases first quickly disposed of, and then my poor fellow was led up.

MEAN AS WERE THE SURROUNDINGS IT MADE A TRAGIC SCENE

"Mean as were the surroundings, I assure you it made a tragic scene. And there the Connecticut lad stood—thinking of the mother who could never bear to hear of shame upon her soldier boy, nor care to hear after where they had made his grave.

"The Captain began the formal questioning; and Billy, in a clear, low voice, answered. Asked if he knew what it meant to converse with the enemy, he said:

"'Yes, sir.'

"'Had he reversed his gun?'

"'Yes, sir.'

"'Had he handed the enemy a package?'

"'Yes, sir.'

"'What did it contain?'

"'Tobacco, sir.'

"Billy whitened again, but he did not lie; and I seemed to read in the depths of his blue eyes a thought of 'mother.' There was a brief pause, and then I knew my moment had come. From my coat-pocket I produced a packet of the tobacco sent by our Northern contractor.

"'Forbes.'

"'Yes, sir.'

"'Was the tobacco you gave the enemy like this?' I spoke, breaking a deathlike stillness.

"Billy's lips quivered. His look was like Cæsar's 'Et tu, Brute!' But he did not flinch. Honest eye and proudly uplifted head were there when he answered, 'Yes, sir.'

"'Captain Hubert,' I observed, turning to my superior, 'there is a cart-load of the stuff still unused, for the reason that this tobacco was condemned as unfit, owing to some poisonous substance in the blue paper wrappers. I need scarcely point out to you,' I continued, 'that sentence of death could only be passed on Forbes for "carrying aid or comfort to the enemy." Now, then, Captain, if you will kindly fill your pipe from this package, I feel sure you will decide whether Forbes can be condemned to death for providing the Johnnies with comfort from old Briggs's consignment.'

"The tension was too great for even a smile, and Captain Hubert's face flushed scarlet. He put out his hand, then drew it back. 'This being the case,' said he, in a stifled voice and rising to his feet, 'we—we—can consider the case dismissed!'

"I met Billy a moment or two later, standing like a statue near my quarters. He looked at me piteously; but when I held out my hand, did not at once take it.

"'Lieutenant,' said he, with the queer smile in his honest eyes I somehow felt he'd learned from his mother, 'I—I—God bless you, sir; but did you send me with poison to those poor chaps?' His voice shook, but he held up his head proudly. 'Killing them in battle, sir, would be fair and square—'

"'Billy,' said I, 'give me your hand, and you'll get your shoulder-straps before the week is out! No, my boy! I picked out papers that hadn't a speck of white stain on them. No, you're not a murderer, my poor Billy; and go to your tent and write to your mother, for we're near a battle harder than the one you and I fought this morning, thanks to the papers from the enemy.'"

"Oh, General!" exclaimed Molly, "and what happened then?"

"Why, my child, Billy went home on a furlough six months later Captain Forbes, if you please, and at present he owns a fine country grocery, from which the apples you're eating this minute have just come, as they do every year regularly, and not once but he encloses a big packet of tobacco marked, 'Not dangerous, General, even to the enemy!'"

V
THE BLOCKADE-RUNNER

A Dangerous Prize

"NOW, Lieutenant, the yarn," said I, as I settled myself comfortably. A heavy sea was running; night had fallen; we were off watch, and snugly stowed between decks, with our legs under the gun-room table, and—jollier still—Lieutenant Bracetaut had promised a yarn. He looked musingly at the oscillating lantern above our heads, and then made a beginning:

"It was not in these days of iron pots, cheese-boxes, and steam-engines, you must know," said he; "but on the dear old frigate Florida—requiescat in pace!—without her mate before a stiff breeze, and with more rats in her hold than in a North Sea whaler. We were the flag-ship of the African squadron. Prize-money was scarce, and the days frightfully hot; when just as the day dropped at the close of September, we were overjoyed to hear tidings of—"

"All hands on deck if you want a share in this prize!" bawled the boatswain down the companionway; and we ungraciously tumbled up, snapping Bracetaut's yarn without compunction.

"Where is she?"

"What is she?"

"I don't see her."

"There she is to the sou'west," said the cockswain, pointing with his spyglass.

"By Jove, a steamer, too!" cried Bracetaut, delightedly.

"The Great Eastern, stuffed with cotton to her scuppers," suggested Jerry Bloom, commencing a hornpipe; and every one else had some guess as to the character of the strange craft.

CHASING A BLOCKADE-RUNNER
(From a contemporary picture in Harper's Weekly)

"Bracetaut is right," said the Captain of the Petrel, who had been studying her intently with his telescope; "she's a steamer, and a big 'un. But she's not coming out; she's making for the Lights with her best foot foremost."

We were glad to hear it; for even cotton could be foregone for the sake of English rifles, hospital stores, and army stuffs. We cracked on more steam, unfurled the top-gallants, and made all preparations for a short chase. We had been to Philadelphia for coal, and were still fifty knots from our old blockading station on the North Carolina coast, to which we were returning. There was a heavy sea from the tempest of the day before; but the sky was cloudless and the moon unusually bright, and our craft was the swiftest in the squadron; so that, with so much sea-room, we had little doubt of overhauling the stranger before she could reach the protecting guns of Fort Macon. A mere speck at first, the object of our attention grew rapidly bigger as we sped on under the extra head of steam and the straining top-gallants. She enlarged against the sky until she grew as big as a whale, and in a few moments we distinguished the column of black smoke which her low chimneys trailed against the sky; but she seemed to have little canvas stretched. Indeed, the gale was yet so strong that any extensive spread of sail was imprudent.

"See what you make of her, Bracetaut," said the Captain, handing his telescope to the weather-worn seaman. "I would be sure that she's none of our own."

"Clyde-built all over," mused the Lieutenant, with his eye to the tube. "No one but a Cockney could have planted her masts; and her jib has the Bristol cut. She sees you and is doing her best. I doubt if you catch her."

"We'll see about that," retorted the skipper. "Let out the studdin' sails! trim the jib!" he roared through his trumpet. "I'll spread every rag if we scrape the sky! More head if possible, Jones," he added; and the engineer went below to see what could be done.

The gale was strong, and her head of steam was already great; but we soon seemed to leap from crest to crest under the stimulus of replenished fires, and the masts fairly bowed beneath their press of canvas. Everybody was agog with excitement, and half the seamen were in the rigging gazing ahead and speculating as to the vessel and her contents.

"Try her with the big bow-chaser, Captain," suggested the Lieutenant; and the order was immediately given.

Boom! went the huge piece, as we quivered on the summit of a lofty wave, and the rushing bolt flashed a phosphorescent light from a dozen crests ere its course was lost in the distance.

"No, go! it's a good three miles," growled Captain Butler, measuring the interval once more with his glass.

"Let me try," said Bracetaut, quietly taking his stand behind the gun, which was now being charged anew, and carefully adjusting the screws.

Again the sullen thunder spouted from the port, and we marked the ball by its path of fire.

"Gone again," grumbled the skipper. "We're paving the floor of the sea with—Ha!" For an instant the messenger had vanished like its predecessor; then, far away to the south, there sprang a fountain of spray—its last dip in the brine—and the mizzen-mast of the stranger snapped short off at the cross-trees, and dragged a cloud of useless canvas down her shrouds.

"Brave shot!" exclaimed the Captain. "Try again, Lieutenant."

"'Try, try again,'" sang that limb of a middy, Jerry Bloom, renewing his hornpipe.

But the rigging of the stranger suddenly grew black with men, the broken spars were cleared away as by magic, another sail puffed out broadly from her foretop to make up for the vanished mizzen-mast, and even as we gazed a strain of band-music came floating over the sea, with the "Bonny blue flag" for its burden.

"She's telling her name," said Bracetaut, laughing.

"Yes, but she's going to kick us," cried Jerry, as a long tongue of flame leaped from the stranger's stern; and the rolling thunder of her gun came to us almost simultaneously with the ball, which whistled through our tops, letting down a heavy splinter on the cockswain's head, who dropped like a dead man, but was only stunned.

It was evident that the stranger was plucky, and not to be taken alive. We still worked on her with our bow-gun, seldom doing much damage, but with the best of intentions; while she kicked off the point of our bowsprit with provoking ease, and burned an ugly hole through our maintop-sail.

"By Jingo! she's growing saucy," said Captain Butler. "Now let me have a shy;" and grasping the piece with a practised hand, he swiftly adjusted it.

"Huzza! I told you so! Clean through her poop!"

Sure enough, the shot struck her after-bulwarks, and must have played hob with the chandeliers in the cabin.

"Just wait till we can give her a broadside," added the winger of the bolt, rubbing his hands good-humoredly.

"We mustn't wait too long, then," said the cool Lieutenant, "for I see the Lookout lights. In half an hour we shall be under the guns of Fort Macon."

He pointed over the side as he spoke, far down the western verge, to a faint, lurid glimmering scarcely brighter than the many stars that surrounded it, but with the hazy lustre which there was no mistaking.

"The rebels are reported to have destroyed the lanterns," said I, suggestively.

"Don't you believe it, my boy," replied the old sailor. "They know when to douse them and when to light a British skipper to their nest."

The chase had now lasted between two and three hours, and the fort at Cape Fear could not be more than twelve miles to our lee. We were still two miles from the stranger, and the chances were momently lessening of overhauling her in time, unless we should succeed in materially disabling her, while our own risk of becoming crippled from her well-directed stern-shots was very great. If the wind had been light the shots in our rigging would have checked our speed but slightly; but the bracing gale that had us in its teeth lent us half our speed, and an unlucky shot in our cross-trees might be irretrievable.

"There! there! we have it now! Was there ever such luck?" cried the Captain, despondently. And our main-sail came down with a rush as he spoke, every one flying from the splinters of the mast, which was severed like a pipe-stem.

We all looked glum enough at this mishap, and began to consider the prize as a might-have-been. But the Captain determined on a last effort, and ordered a broadside volley, though the distance, a mile and a half at least, made success extremely doubtful. The ship rounded to handsomely. The ports were open, twenty cannon were already loaded and manned, and, at the given signal, a long sheet of flame leaped from the side, and the noble frigate roared and quivered to her keelson. Another instant and a wild huzza swelled upward from our crowded deck; for the broadside was a success. The entire rigging of the stranger seemed in ruins; her bowsprit was trailing in the sea; and we could distinguish another ugly smash in her stern, which must have come very near destroying her precious flukes. Of course the prospect was now far better than before, but still by no means certain, as it was questionable whether we were not almost equally disabled in the rigging, and the rapidity with which the damaged tops of the stranger were mended and cleared away seemed miraculous, though she now gave over firing, apparently bent on safety only by sharp sailing.

New spars were already up on our own main-mast, and, with a clew or two on the mizzen-shrouds, and the use of the after-braces, with double duty on the mizzen-top-gallant spars, our main-sail was again aloft, with cheering indications that we were gaining fast. In fifteen minutes we had so sensibly diminished the interval between us and our prey that we ceased firing. But we were over-confident. The lanterns of Cape Lookout were now left far away on our starboard quarter, and every forward furlong we made was so much nearer to the formidable fort. Just then a faint flash, like the horizon glimmer of summer lightning, shone above the waters far beyond the ship we were pursuing, and a hardly heard but ominous boom told us that the old sea-dragon, Fort Macon, was not sleeping in the moonlight. We now renewed our pelting of the stranger with further damage to her tops. Whereupon she veered for Shackleford Shoals, with the evident intention of beaching herself if unable to get under the fort. Another quarter of an hour and we were within long range of the heavy coast-guns of the fortress, which seemed to understand the state of the case perfectly, for shells began to drop around us briskly. And now the great breakers of the sandy coast were plainly discernible on the starboard, tossing their white plumes high above the beach. Here and there a bluff rose from the monotone of sand; and the Devil's Skillet—a dangerous reef—was boiling white a little lower down.

Shackleford Shoals is a low, narrow sand-bank, about twenty miles in length. Its lower extremity comes within three miles, at a rough guess, of the Borden Banks, or Shoals, on the easternmost point of which the fort is situated. The bank is everywhere treacherous, but especially at this southern point, where the danger of the shoals is hidden by apparently deep water. And now as we neared our expected prey, she made a bold push for this inlet; but as we dashed in between her and the fort, regardless of the latter's continuous firing, she altered her course, and steered head-on for the fatal breakers.

"She's bent on suicide!" said Jerry, who then ran below for his pistols, as the Captain ordered the boats to be manned.

"Has she struck?"

"No—yes—there she goes!"

Sure enough, she had grounded and slightly heeled over, but in such deep water that the soft sand of the shoals would not hold her long. Two of our boats were manned, with our beloved Lieutenant as commander of the expedition, and I was in his boat. We pushed off with some difficulty, on account of the heavy sea. As we did so we saw the boats of the blockade-runner also lowered, and pulling inside for the inlet. The rats were leaving the crib.

"You can get her off if you try, Bracetaut. Throw over everything to lighten her," was the parting injunction of Captain Butler, and as we pulled away he hauled his ship out of range of the fort. It was rather uncomfortable the way the shells ducked and plunged around us, or burst above our heads, but we pulled away for the prize. Our boat was the last to reach the ship—a first-class iron propeller, of great tonnage, and clipper-built. As the crew of the advanced boat climbed up her sides several crashes made us aware that the fort was turning her guns against the vessel, to deprive us of the plunder.

"And hot-shot at that. Listen!" said Bracetaut to me; when the fizzing sound of the plunging hot-shot was plainly distinguishable.

Our boat was within a rod of the prize when we perceived the men who had already boarded her jumping hastily over the bulwarks, dropping into their boat, and pushing off, as if something unusual was to pay. One had been left behind. It was the little middy, Jerry Bloom, who now appeared unconcernedly leaning over the side and coolly awaiting the Lieutenant's orders.

"What's her cargo?" bellowed Bracetaut through his trumpet.

"Powder!" sang back the shrill tones of the New World Casabianca, and siz! siz! went the plunging red-hot shot; and crash! crash! they went against the floating magazine with frightful precision.

"Jump for your life!" roared the Lieutenant to Jerry. "Back-water, you lubbers! back, for your lives!"

We saw the midshipman join his palms over his head and leap from the gunwale of the fated ship. Scarcely had his slender figure cut the brine before a number of sharp reports were heard—then a long, deep, volcanic rumbling, that swelled into a terrific thunder, deafened our ears; a dozen columns of blood-red flame shot up to the stars; and we saw the deck and majestic spars of the doomed blockade-runner spring aloft in fragments! A huge black mass descended with a fearful splash a yard from our bows— the long stern-chaser going to the bottom—the sides of the powder-ship yawned wide open an instant, filled with fire, then disappeared, the flames dying out. The sea was ploughed around us by the falling fragments of deck and spar, and the glorious steamer was no more!

VI
TWO DAYS WITH MOSBY

An Adventure with Guerillas

I

I WAS up at reveille. Orders to inspect the camp of dismounted cavalry near Harper's Ferry had been in my pocket two days, while I awaited an escort through the fifty miles of guerilla-infested country which lay between me and that distant post. This was the day for the regular train, and a thousand wagons were expected to leave Sheridan's headquarters, on Cedar Creek, at daylight, with a brigade of infantry as guard, and a troop of cavalry as outriders.

An hour's ride of eight miles along a picketed line across the valley brought me to the famous "Valley Pike," and near the headquarters of the army. Torbert was there, and I awaited his detailed instructions. Unavoidable delay ensued. Despatches were to be sent, and they were not yet ready. An hour passed, and, meantime the industrious wagon-train was lightly and rapidly rolling away down the pike. The last wagon passed out of sight, and the rear-guard closed up behind it before I was ready to start. No other train was to go for four days. I must overtake this one or give up my journey. At length, accompanied by a single orderly, and my colored servant, George Washington, a contraband, commonly called "Wash," I started in pursuit of the train.

As I had nearly passed Newtown I overtook a small party apparently from the rear-guard of the train, who were lighting their pipes and buying cakes and apples at a small grocery on the right of the pike. They seemed to be in charge of a non-commissioned officer.

"Good-morning, Sergeant. You had better close up at once. The train is getting well ahead, and this is the favorite beat of Mosby."

"All right, sir," he replied with a smile, and nodding to his men, they mounted at once and closed in behind me, while quite to my surprise I noticed in front of me three more of the party whom I had not before seen.

An instinct of danger seized me. I saw nothing to justify it, but I felt a presence of evil which I could not shake off. The men were in Union blue complete, and wore on their caps the well-known Greek cross which distinguishes the gallant Sixth Corps. They were young, intelligent, cleanly, and good-looking soldiers, armed with revolvers and Spencer's repeating carbine. I noticed the absence of sabres, but the presence of the Spencer, which was a comparatively new arm in our service, reassured me, and I thought it impossible that the enemy could as yet be possessed of them.

We galloped on merrily, and just as I was ready to laugh at my own fears, "Wash," who had been riding behind me and had heard some remark made by the soldiers, brushed up to my side, and whispered through his teeth, chattering with fear:

"Massa, Secesh, sure! Run like de debbel!"

I turned to look back at these words, and saw six carbines levelled at me at twenty paces distant, and the Sergeant, who had watched every motion of the negro, came riding towards me with revolver drawn and the sharp command, "Halt! Surrender!"

We had reached a low place where the Opequan Creek crosses the pike, a mile from Newtown. The train was not a quarter of a mile ahead, but out of sight for the moment over the west ridge.

High stone-walls lined the pike on either side, and a narrow bridge across the stream was in front of me and already occupied by the three rascals who had acted as advance-guard, who now coolly turned round and raised their carbines.

I remembered the military maxim, a mounted man should never surrender until his horse is disabled. I hesitated an instant considering what I should do, and quite in doubt whether I was myself or some other fellow whom I had read of as captured and hung by guerillas; but at the repetition of the sharp command, aided by the revolver thrust into my face, I concluded I was undoubtedly the other fellow and surrendered accordingly.

My sword and revolver were taken at once by the Sergeant, who proved to be a rebel lieutenant in disguise, and who remarked, laughing as he took them:

"We closed up, Captain, as you directed; as this is a favorite beat of Mosby's, I hope our drill was satisfactory."

"All right, Sergeant. Every dog has his day, and yours happens to come now. Possibly my turn may come to-morrow."

"Your turn to be hung," he replied.

II

It was not long before I was ushered into the presence of John S. Mosby, Lieutenant-Colonel, C. S. A.

He stood a little apart from his men, by the side of a splendid gray horse, with his right hand grasping the bridle-rein and resting on the pommel of his saddle—a slight, medium-sized man, sharp of feature, quick of sight, lithe of limb, with a bronzed face of the color and tension of whip-cord. His hair, beard, and mustache were light brown in color. His large, well-shaped head showed a high forehead, deep-set gray eyes, a straight Grecian nose, a firm mouth, and large ears. His whole expression told of energy, hard service, and—love of whiskey. He wore top-boots, and a civilian's overcoat, black, lined with red, and beneath it the complete gray uniform of a Confederate Lieutenant-Colonel, with its two stars on the side of the standing collar, and the whole surmounted by the inevitable slouched hat of the whole Southern race. His men were about half in blue and half in butternut.

Mosby, after taking my horse and quietly examining my papers, presently looked up with a peculiar gleam of satisfaction on his face.

"Ah, Captain B——! Inspector-General of ——'s Cavalry! Good-morning, Captain! Glad to see you, sir! Indeed, there is but one I would prefer to see this morning to yourself, and that is your commander. Were you present, sir, the other day at the hanging of eight of my men as guerillas at Front Royal?"

I answered him firmly, "I was present, sir; and, like you, have only to regret that it was not the commander instead of his unfortunate men."

This answer seemed to please Mosby, for he apparently expected a denial. He assumed a grim smile, and directed Lieutenant Whiting to search me.

My gold hunting-watch and chain, several rings, a set of shirt-studs and sleeve-buttons, a Masonic pin, some coins, and about three hundred dollars in greenbacks, with some letters and pictures of the dear ones at home, and a small pocket Bible, were taken. My cavalry boots, worth about fifteen dollars, were apprised at six hundred and fifty in Confederate money; my watch at three thousand dollars, and the other articles in about the same proportion, including my poor servant "Wash," who was put in and raffled for at two thousand dollars, so that my entire outfit made quite a respectable prize.

"Wash" was very indignant that he should be thought worth only two thousand dollars, Confederate money, and informed them that he considered himself unappreciated, and that, among other accomplishments, he could make the best milk-punch of any man in the Confederacy.

When all this was concluded, Mosby took me a little one side and returned to me the pocket Bible, the letters and pictures, and the Masonic pin, saying quietly as he did so, alluding to the latter with a significant sign:

"You may as well keep this. It may be of use to you somewhere."

I thanked him warmly for his kindness as I took his offered hand, and really began to think Mosby almost a gentleman and a soldier, although he had just robbed me in the most approved manner of modern highwaymen.

Immediate preparations were made for the long road to Richmond and Libby Prison. A guard of fifteen men, in command of Lieutenant Whiting, was detailed as our escort, and, accompanied by Mosby himself, we started directly across the country, regardless of roads, in an easterly direction towards the Shenandoah and the Blue Ridge.

We were now in company of nine more of our men, who had been taken at different times, making eleven of our party in all, besides the indignant contraband "Wash," whom it was thought prudent also to send to the rear for safe-keeping.

I had determined to escape if even half an opportunity should present itself, and the boys were quick in understanding my purpose, and intimating their readiness to risk their lives in the attempt. One of them in particular, George W. M'Cauley, commonly known as Mack, and another one named Brown, afterwards proved themselves heroes.

At Howettsville on the Shenandoah, nine miles below Front Royal, we bivouacked for the night in an old school-house.

Our party of eleven were assigned to one side of the lower floor of the school-house, where we lay down side by side with our heads to the wall and our feet nearly meeting the feet of the guard, who lay in the same manner opposite us, with their heads to the other wall, except three, who formed a relief guard for the sentry's post at the door.

Above the head of the guard along the wall ran a low desk, on which each man of them placed his carbine and revolver before disposing himself for sleep.

A fire before the door dimly lighted the room; and the scene as the men dropped gradually to sleep has stamped itself upon my memory like a picture of war painted by Rembrandt.

I had taken care to place myself between M'Cauley and Brown, and the moment the rebels began to snore and the sentry to nod over his pipe, we were in earnest and deep conversation.

M'Cauley proposed to warn the others and make a simultaneous rush for the carbines, and take our chances of stampeding the guard and escaping. But on passing the word in a whisper along our line, only three men were found willing to join us. As the odds were so largely against us, it was in vain to urge the subject.

The march began at an early hour the next morning, and the route ran directly up the Blue Ridge. We had emerged from the forest and ascended about one-third of the height of the mountain, when the full valley became visible, spread out like a map before us, showing plainly the lines of our army, its routes of supply, its foraging parties out, and my own camp at Front Royal as distinctly as if we stood in one of its streets.

We now struck a wood-path running southward and parallel with the ridge of the mountains, along which we travelled for hours, with this wonderful panorama of forest and river, mountain and plain before us in all the gorgeous beauty of the early autumn.

"This is a favorite promenade of mine," said Mosby. "I love to see your people sending out their almost daily raids after me. There comes one of them now almost towards us. If you please, we will step behind the point and see them pass. It may be the last sight you will have of your old friends for some time," and, looking in the direction he pointed, I saw a squadron of my own regiment coming directly towards us on a road running under the foot of the mountain, and apparently on some foraging expedition down the valley. They passed within a half-mile of us, under the mountain, while Mosby stood with folded arms on a rock above them.

Before noon we reached the road running through Manassas Gap, which was held by about one hundred of Mosby's men, who signalled him as he approached, and here, much to my regret, the great guerilla left us, bidding me a kindly good-bye.

We were hurried through the gap and down the eastern side of the Blue Ridge, and by three o'clock reached Chester Gap, after passing which we descended into the valley and moved rapidly towards Sperryville on the direct line to Richmond.

III

As we were far within the Confederate lines, our guard was reduced to Lieutenant Whiting and three men, and our party of eleven prisoners had seven horses among them. There was also a pack-horse carrying our forage, rations, and some blankets. To the saddle of this pack-horse were strapped two Spencer carbines, muzzle downward, with their accoutrements complete, including two well-filled cartridge-boxes.

I called Mack's attention to this fact as soon as the guard was reduced, and he needed no second hint to comprehend its full significance. He soon after dismounted, and when it came his turn to mount again, he selected, apparently by accident, the poorest and most broken-down horse of the party. After this he seemed to find it very difficult to keep up, and in some mysterious way he actually succeeded in laming his horse.

He then dropped back to the Lieutenant in charge and modestly asked to exchange his lame horse for the pack-horse. He was particularly winning in his address, and his request was at once granted, without a suspicion of its object or a thought of the fatal carbines on the pack-saddle. I used some little skill in diverting the attention of the Lieutenant while the pack was readjusted; and as the rain had begun to fall freely, no one of the guard was particularly alert.

I was presently gratified with the sight of Mack riding ahead on the pack-horse, with the two carbines still strapped to the saddle, but loosened, and well concealed by his heavy poncho, which he had spread as protection from the rain. These carbines were seven-shooters, loaded from the breech by simply drawing out from the hollow stock a spiral spring, and dropping in the seven cartridges, one after the other, and then inserting the spring again behind them, which coils as it is pressed home, and by its elasticity forces the cartridges forward, one at a time, into the barrel at the successive action of the lock.

I could follow the movements of Mack's right arm underneath the poncho. While he was guiding his horse with his left hand, looking the other way, and chatting glibly with the other boys, I distinctly saw him draw the springs from those carbines with his right hand and hook them into the upper button-hole of his coat to support them, while he dropped in the cartridges one after another, trotting his horse at the time to conceal the noise of their click, and finally forcing down the springs. Then the brave fellow glanced at me triumphantly.

I nodded approval. Fearing that Mack might act too hastily, yet knowing that any instant might lead to discovery, I rode carelessly across the road to Brown, who was on foot, and, dismounting, asked him to tighten my girth.

Then I told him the situation as quietly as possible, and requested him to ride up gradually beside Mack, to communicate with him, and, at a signal from me, to seize one of the carbines and do his duty as a soldier if he valued his liberty.

Brown was terribly frightened and trembled like a leaf, but went immediately to his post, and I did not doubt would do his duty well.

I rode up again to the side of Lieutenant Whiting, and like an echo from the past came back to me my words of yesterday, "Possibly my turn may come to-morrow."

I engaged him in conversation, and, among other things, spoke of the prospect of sudden death as one always present in our army life, and the tendency it had to either harden or soften the character according to the quality of the individual.

He expressed the opinion which many hold, that a brutal man is made more brutal by it, and a refined and cultivated man is softened.

We were on the immediate flank of Early's army. His cavalry was all around us. The road was much used. It was almost night. We had passed a rebel picket but a mile back, and knew not how near another camp might be.

The three rebel guards were riding in front of us and on our flanks. Our party of prisoners was in the centre, and I was by the side of Lieutenant Whiting, who acted as rear-guard, when we entered a small copse of willows which for a moment covered the road. The hour was propitious. I gave the fatal signal and instantly threw myself from my saddle upon the Lieutenant, grasping him around the arms and dragging him from his horse, in the hope of securing his revolver, capturing him, and compelling him to pilot us outside of the rebel lines. At the same instant Mack raised one of the loaded carbines, and, in less time than I can write it, shot two of the guard in front of him, killing them instantly; and then coolly turning in his saddle, and seeing me struggling in the road with the Lieutenant, and the chances of obtaining the revolver apparently against me, he raised the carbine the third time; and as I strained the now desperate rebel to my breast, with his livid face over my left shoulder, he shot him as directly between the eyes as if firing at a target at ten paces distance.

Brown had only wounded his man in the side, and allowed him to escape.

Our position was now perilous. Not a man of us knew the country, except in a general way. The rebel camps could not be far away; the whole country would be alarmed in an hour, darkness was intervening; and I doubted not that, before sundown, blood-hounds as well as men would be on our track.

One-half our party had already scattered, panic-stricken, at the first alarm, and they were flying through the country in every direction.

Only five remained, including the faithful Wash, who immediately showed his practical qualities by searching the bodies of the slain, and recovering, among other things, my gold hunting-watch from the person of Lieutenant Whiting, and over eleven hundred dollars in greenbacks, the proceeds, doubtless, of their various robberies of our men.

"Not quite nuff," said Wash, showing his ivories from ear to ear. "Dey vally dis nigger at two thousand dollars. I tink I ought to git de money."

We instantly mounted the best horses, and, well armed with carbines and revolvers, struck directly for the mountain on our right; but knowing that would be the first place we should be sought for, we soon changed our direction to the south, and rode for hours as rapidly as we could ride, directly towards the enemy. Before darkness came on we had made thirty miles from the place of our escape; and then turning sharply up the mountain, we rode as far as horses could climb, and, abandoning them, pushed on through the whole night to the very summit of the Blue Ridge. There we could see the rebel camp-fires in the valley, and at break of dawn we could view their entire lines.

The length of this weary day, and the terrible pangs of hunger and thirst which we suffered on this barren mountain, belong to the mere common experience of a soldier's life, and I need not describe them here.

We had to go still farther south to avoid the scouts and pickets, and finally struck the Shenandoah twenty miles to the rear of Early's entire army. There we built a raft, and floated by night forty miles down that memorable stream, through his crafty pickets, until the glorious old flag once more greeted us in welcome.

VII
THE FIRST TIME UNDER FIRE

The Experience of a Raw Recruit

WHEN the President ordered the army to be filled up by recruiting, drafting, or otherwise, and the peaceful moneyed men of the North were roused to protect their persons by draining their pockets, I was moved by love of country, of adventure, and three hundred dollars, to offer myself as a recruit in the —— Cavalry Regiment. So, under the protection of a strong body of infantry, I and fifty others were first jolted forty miles on a cattle-car, then marched twenty-five miles to corps headquarters, then fifteen across country to our brigadier-commander, and then back again near the place whence we started to the camp of the regiment. After accompanying on foot the movements of our mounted troops for the next three weeks, it suddenly occurred to some member of the General's staff that we might perhaps be more efficient on horseback; and so we were transported back on the cars to the Cavalry Depot at Washington to be provided with horses. As we were all stout, active young fellows, we lost in these various movements only fifteen men from disease, desertion, and capture by guerillas, and only five or six others got disheartened, and escaped home on our passage through the city; so in three weeks more thirty of us, well-mounted, armed, and equipped, rejoined our command, and were reported fit for duty.

About a fortnight after this the squadron was called in from picket, and marched rapidly to unite with the regiment which was engaged with the enemy. As we drew near, the firing became sharper and sharper, and suddenly the captain commanding formed us in line, and carried us forward on a trot. The rapidity of the movement, the jingling of the accoutrements, the pressure of the horses and men on each side of me caused a sensation of excitement rather pleasant than otherwise, and I began to feel very brave and warlike.

"What is it?" asked I of the old soldier beside me. "Are we going to charge them right off?"

I shall never forget the look of contemptuous wonder with which he looked at me as he replied:

"I've been jest two years in this here regiment, and you're the first man I ever met who thought he was going a-charging without drawing sabres. We're agoing to be shot at, young feller. That's all for the present."

There was something so cold-blooded in this that my enthusiasm was suddenly checked. I asked no more questions until we were halted behind a thin belt of woods. On the other side active skirmishing was going on. Here I saw the old soldiers get their carbines in readiness, and snap the caps to clear the tubes. The consciousness of the deadly earnest in which the weapons were soon to be used turned me sick for the moment, and made me think of home and of death. All the time there were curious sounds in the air above our heads, as if large night-beetles had mistaken us for lighted candles, and were whirring around us; but as the others took no notice of them I hesitated to speak. At last, seeing the old soldier who had answered me dodge down quickly as one of these sounds was heard close above him, I ventured to inquire what sort of bugs those were that made such a noise? Indignation blended with scorn was visible in his countenance as he satisfied my curiosity:

"Bugs! Do you think that I am such a skeery old woman as to be twisting myself in my saddle 'cause a bug was flying at me? Them's pisen, them are! Them's bullets!"

If he had told me they were fifteen-inch shells he couldn't have startled and astonished me more. Here I had been in imminent danger for ten minutes, and I had not known anything about it. Instinctively I debated whether I could get out of the way without being detected and disgraced, and the same impulse turned my eyes towards my Captain. There he sat, as cool as a cucumber, reading a man a lecture as to the proper method of advancing his carbine, forcing two or three others to dress themselves more accurately upon the right sergeant, and all the while looking straight at me. There was no use in my trying to dodge away then.

Presently a horse in front of me reared a little and dropped to the ground, and one or two men on foot came straggling through the wood from the front. Then there came slowly forth a mounted man leaning forward on his saddle, his hand pressed to his side, and red with blood. Then a squad of ten or fifteen burst through the branches, slinging their empty carbines, and rallying in a disorderly fashion upon our flank. With a deadlier fury the whir of the bullets swept above our line. "Steady there, men!" sang out the Captain. "Get your carbines ready, boys!" An old infantry soldier, who was my front rank man, turned round to me, and said, "I say, you take care to fire over my head, and don't blow my brains out with your shooting, d'ye hear?" I was in the act of promising to pay the most exact attention to his order, when I was startled by a burst of laughter behind me. That ubiquitous Captain was there listening. "Fire over your head, you goose!" he exclaimed. "I don't want him to bring down a star or a turkey-buzzard. You keep your fire, Dan, until I tell you to shoot; and don't let me see a man in the rear rank fire while I keep him standing there. Mind that now."

While he was talking I could tell from the shouts that our men had repelled the rebel charge, and I was able to bear with composure the sight of a dead officer carried sadly past us by some of his men. Then all at once along the enemy's line crashed a volley, lighting up the closing night with a glare of fire whose length startled and amazed me. Horses fell on either side of me, and here and there a man's face would change, and he would slide from his saddle or draw his horse back from the line. It was dreadful sitting there inactive, waiting helplessly for death; and my hand half-consciously drawing upon my rein, my horse fell back about a foot from his place in line. At that instant the Captain cried out, "Attention, there!" and looking round, I saw his eyes fixed on me again. Again he cried, "Attention! Squadron into single rank, march!" and as I obeyed the order I saw our skirmishers slowly falling back through the wood and forming a line upon our extreme left and in our rear. Then there was a pause.

Presently I saw a movement among the trees, and I could make out a mass of men clustering together just upon their edge. With a thrill, I knew that for the first time I saw the enemy; and every sensation was merged in a frantic desire to shoot, while every nerve within my body was quivering with excitement. Then the Captain's voice, steady and cheerful, sounded along the line, with some sympathetic power calming my shaking nerves and making every muscle as firm as iron. "Ready! Aim low. Front rank men, fire!" A blaze of light ran along our line, there was a deafening explosion, and a blinding smoke, through which I could hear the bullets of the enemy as they whistled past. I could see nothing, but I heard the voice of the Captain from my right command, "Rear rank men, fire!" and as our second volley crashed out, there came the order, "Load and fire at will." And now it was crack! crack! as fast as we could get the cartridges into our guns, shouting and cheering as we did so, in answer to the rebel yells. At length our shouts met no response. I heard the officer's command, "Cease firing!" the smoke swept away, and I found it was black night, through which I could just see that I was one of about forty men, the remnant of the squadron. I could hear a few slowly trotting back to the rear. I could make out others on foot crossing the hill-top beyond, and could see a mass of dead horses and one or two dead men still lying at my feet. For a few minutes the Captain let us remove the corpses and destroy the equipments of the dead animals, and then we withdrew triumphantly to our comrades, the Captain telling us once that we had done well, and then bewailing his fate that he commanded men who did not know how to wheel by fours. That was my first acquaintance with rebel bullets, and even the old soldiers said that it was the closest affair in which they had ever been engaged.

Two days afterwards I heard, for the first time, the sound of a shell; and I might as well make a clean breast of it, once for all, by describing my sensations.

We were in the rear of the army as it fell back upon Centreville, formed in line as a reserve. The rest of the cavalry had moved on after the infantry, leaving us to hold a hill from which the enemy might have annoyed them with artillery. We sat there without seeing anything in particular, wondering why the rebels did not come out of the woods beyond us; when suddenly there was a big puff of smoke at the edge of the trees, a loud bang, and a tremendous screech in the air above our heads, so close that the sound almost took my head off. I looked at the Captain, expecting to hear him say, "By fours, do something or other"; but he only said, "Steady!" as there was another puff, another bang, and another screech, as a big black mass of iron struck the ground ten yards in front of us, bounded over our heads, and burst almost above us. It gave such a shock to my nerves that I could not do anything but shake, and I felt as if I should have much preferred to be under the ground rather than above it.

Those rebels banged away at us for half a dozen rounds, each time striking close to us, before I saw our skirmish-line come riding back at a walk, and heard the Captain give the order, "By fours, march! Right counter-march!" and back we started. Two files in front of me marched Dan E—, one of those fellows who always has his retort ready. I heard the man next to him scolding at Dan's crowding him out of place: "Why can't you follow your file-leader?" "Hang the file-leader," answered Dan, pushing him harder yet; "they've got the range of him." And as he spoke a shell came down and buried itself in the earth just where he would have been if he had kept in his place. I need not say that we all turned aside after that, and pretty soon we got safely out of reach.

Now I know what artillery and musketry are both like; and I sincerely hope that I shall not face it again.

VIII
HOW CUSHING DESTROYED THE "ALBEMARLE"

One of the Bravest Deeds in Naval History

IT is the night of October 27, 1864. A blockading fleet of Union vessels rides at anchor off the harbor of Plymouth, North Carolina. Alongside the flag-ship an open launch is secured, her after-part made visible to those on board the over-towering ship owing to the glow that comes from the open door of the little furnace. The light that streams forth also throws into relief the face and form of the engineer as he spreads a layer of "green" coals over the surface of the fire, and thrusts the slender brass spout of his oil-can into the various feed-cups of the machinery. Just abaft the cockpit, holding the stern of the launch to the frigate by means of a boat-hook, stands a blue-jacket, his naked feet showing as two white patches on the lead-colored planks. Another seaman is performing a similar office forward in the bow, while several more are gathered about a long, curious-looking spar carefully secured, with its cylinder-shaped head resting on a wad of cotton-waste; but these men are lost to view, owing to the gloom of their situation, which is deepened by contrast to the firelight aft. At the open gangway of the flag-ship two officers stand conversing. Beside them a gray-haired quartermaster is stationed, lantern in hand, to light the way down the ladder that leads to the launch. In the shoulder-straps of one of the officers glistens a single silver star, which denotes his Commodore's rank, while the two gold bars that decorate the straps of the other show him to be a Lieutenant. As the latter is observed in the rays of the lantern, his smooth face and slender figure are suggestive rather of extreme youth than of a man qualified by years and experience to assume the office that his uniform represents. The gold bands around his coat sleeves have been nobly won, however, and the boy of nineteen, who entered the service three years previous as a master's mate, has already commanded with singular and enviable distinction a gun-boat of the blockading squadron. There is a touch of fatherly tenderness and a depth of anxiety in the old Commodore's voice as he speaks:

"Cushing, my boy, you are going to almost certain death; the rebels have learned of your object, and are prepared for the attempt. The Albemarle, as you know, is surrounded with heavy floating timbers so arranged that you cannot get within thirty feet of her, and unless you can succeed in laying your boat alongside, how can you expect to explode the torpedo?"

The lines of the Lieutenant's thinly cut mouth deepen, and the brows draw ominously down over the flashing eyes.

"Commodore, I've got my plan all worked out, and I'll carry it through or die with it! If I don't succeed in destroying that iron-clad, she will come out here before long, and perhaps sink the fleet. It's worth the risk, sir, and I'm willing to take it along with my volunteer crew." Then, as his natural spirit of recklessness and humor comes to the surface for a moment, he smiles and continues, "It's either another stripe or death, Commodore."

The flag-officer presses the young man's hand, while he says, huskily, "God bless and grant you success and a safe return!"

Preceded by the quartermaster, Lieutenant Cushing descends the gangway ladder and drops into the launch.

"Lieutenant," says the old man, "there won't be no sleep in the fleet to-night; if ye'll hexcuse the liberty, sir, I'll be a-prayin' for ye."

"All right, Lynch; but pray hard, for I'll need it," replies Cushing. Then he looks at the face of the little dial which registers the steam-pressure, and turns to the engineer: "Keep a full head of steam up, but be careful not to let her get so much that she will open the safety-valve and let Johnny know we're coming." Next he goes forward, examines the torpedo-spar, stations his small crew, orders the furnace door closed, and lays hold of the steering-wheel in the forward cockpit. "Shove off," he orders.

The great black hull of the flag-ship slips into the gloom ahead. A moment later the propeller churns the water, the tiller is put over to port, the head of the launch swerves to starboard, and is kept steadily pointed towards Plymouth, where lies the great rebel iron-clad Albemarle, waiting only for the time, speedily coming, when, with equipment complete, she will steam out to do battle with the wooden walls of her enemies.

After the fleet has been left well astern, the boyish commander orders the engines stopped, and calls the men around him.

"Boys," he says, "I'm going to tell you my plan, so that you may work it out, if possible, in case anything happens to me when we get under fire. As soon as I make out the ship and get my bearings, I'm going to put on a full head of steam, and jump the launch over the logs that surround her on the water side. Once over the spars, it will be only a few feet between us and the hull; so we must have the torpedo ready to push under the water against her side as soon as we get near enough. On the dock that she is moored to they have a couple of howitzers and a company of sharp-shooters to help guard the approach from sea, and on board they are sure to be prepared to give us a warm welcome. I will keep the wheel until we are over the logs, then I will handle the torpedo, so see that it is clear for me. But if I should fall, try to carry out my plan, then jump overboard, dive under the logs, swim across the river, and make your way down along the bank until you get abreast of the fleet, where you can signal. That is all, except to strip yourselves for a swim. Do you understand?"

"Ay, ay, sir, we understand," comes the answer from the handful of heroes.

The little wheel under the stern of the launch turns over slowly and noiselessly as eager, anxious eyes peer ahead into the night.

Suddenly a huge blot is made out a little on the port bow, and a moment later it shapes itself into the outlines of a dock with a great vessel lying alongside.

Out of the gloom rings the challenge, "Boat ahoy!"

While the echo of the last word trembles, Cushing orders, fiercely: "Give it to her! Steady, boys!"

The engineer opens wide the valve, and throws the wild pressure of a full head of steam into the cylinder. The launch jumps forward in time to escape a shower of iron hail that ploughs into her white wake.

Before the guns can be pointed anew a long, narrow barrier washing level with the water shows a few feet ahead.

A sheet of flame from the rifle-barrels on the dock and ship, so close to the open boat that it scorches the air in the faces of the crew, makes vivid for an instant the onrushing destroyer. One of the blue-jackets throws his arms up, and falls face downward in the cockpit just as the stem of the launch strikes the log.

Will she go over it? is the agonizing thought of the brave youth who stands in the very bosom of the deadly tempest.

The head of the boat rears itself on the air until the water is splashing into the stern-sheets aft; then, without checking her mad rush, she clears the barrier like a steeple-chaser and hurls herself forward.

Another volley greets them, and the engineer and one more of the sailors go down; but Lieutenant Cushing springs from the wheel, grasps the torpedo-spar, and as the bow of the launch strikes the rebel ram he thrusts it against her side just as a thick storm of missiles from the howitzers crashes into his boat and shatters it to pieces.

But the doom of the Albemarle is written. An awful rumbling is heard, accompanied by the sound of splintering timbers, followed by a towering volume of torn and maddened waters that for a moment hide the scene from friend and foe, and under cover of which Lieutenant Cushing regains the river beyond the floating logs.

Mingled shouts of command and cries of rage are heard by the swimmer when he comes to the surface after his plunge under the barrier. A number of bullets whistle above his head and patter into the water around him. It is evident that he is yet within the range of vision of the sharp-shooters, so he draws a long breath and sinks below the level again, striking out strong, and swimming until forced to regain the air.

The confusion of voices is yet audible, but when he turns his eyes in the direction of the clamor nothing is visible save the indistinct outline of the shore; then he knows that he no longer affords a mark for the soldiers on the dock.

But another cause of alarm is quickly manifest, for he catches the sound of the thud of oars as they pound against the rowlocks, telling him that the enemy have manned a boat and are seeking him. Before he can decide as to the direction in which to swim in order to get out of the track of the on-coming craft, it looms up only a few yards from him.

There is only one course to pursue, so, catching a quick breath, he quietly sinks, and the boat passes over the spot where the bubbles on the water mark his disappearance.

Until he experiences a sense of suffocation he remains under, swimming off at right angles to the path of his seekers, so that his head may not be in line with the eyes of the rowers when he regains the surface.

When he again casts his anxious eyes around, nothing is seen, so he throws himself on his back and floats while recovering his strength, and shortly after strikes out for the opposite bank of the river, which he reaches after a weary trial, then creeps into the underbrush, and sleeps from exhaustion.

The sun is high when he awakes. Parting the wild foliage, he looks across and up the stream at the scene of his exploit. The dock is plainly to be seen, but the Albemarle has disappeared. Looking intently, he sees two masts rising from the water near the pier, and is thus assured that the career of the rebel ship is ended.

Ha! What causes that rustling of the foliage to his right? Is it an animal, or is it an enemy in search of him?

Almost naked, and altogether defenceless, he watches breathlessly.

He promises himself that he will never be taken alive. Better to die than to endure the tortures of a Southern prison. The bushes part a little further, and a man's sun-browned face and brawny bare shoulders and tattooed arms come into view.

"Jack!" says the Lieutenant, in a loud, glad whisper.

"Lieutenant!" responds the seaman, in a tone of equal surprise and gladness.

All day the officer and his companion, the only survivors of the expedition, work their way painfully through the swamp, and just as the sun is sinking they drag their bare, bleeding feet and cruelly lacerated bodies out on the bank of the river opposite the Union fleet.

All hands have been called to "make sunset," and the men are silently standing by the signal halyards and boat-falls waiting for the word of command, when the quartermaster on the bridge of the flag-ship quickly levels his telescope at the shore, then hurriedly approaches and addresses the officer of the deck, who stands beside the Captain. The latter takes the glass from the seaman, peers through it for an instant, wheels sharply around, and speaks to the Lieutenant.

"Away, first cutter!" roars the latter.

The boatswain's mate blows a shrill pipe, and repeats the order.

"Go down the boat-falls, boys; lively's the word! Jump into the cutter, Mr. Arnold, and pull into the beach for the men!"

Half an hour later Lieutenant Cushing comes over the gangway and salutes the Commodore. "I report my return on board with one man, sir," he says; "the Albemarle is destroyed."

IX
PRESIDENT LINCOLN AND THE SLEEPING SENTINEL

I

THE story of President Lincoln and the sleeping sentinel offers certain substantial facts which are common to all its versions. A soldier named Scott, condemned to be shot for the crime of sleeping on his post, was pardoned by President Lincoln, only to be killed afterwards at the battle of Lee's Mills, on the Peninsula. The incidental facts are varied according to the taste, the fancy, or the imagination of the writer of each version. The number of persons who claim to have procured the intervention of the President to save the life of the soldier nearly equals that of the different versions. As these persons worked independently of each other, and one did not know what another had done, it is not improbable that several of them are entitled to some measure of credit, of which I should be most unwilling to deprive them.

The story of this young soldier, as it was presented to me, so touchingly reveals some of the kindlier qualities of the President's character that it seldom fails to charm those to whom it is related. I shall give its facts as I understand them, and I think I can guarantee their general accuracy.

On a dark September morning in 1861, when I reached my office, I found waiting there a party of soldiers, none of whom I knew personally. They were greatly excited, all speaking at the same time, and they were consequently unintelligible. One of them wore the bars of a Captain. I said to them, pleasantly, "Boys, I cannot understand you. Pray, let your Captain say what you want and what I can do for you." They complied, and the Captain put me in possession of the following facts:

They belonged to the Third Vermont Regiment, raised, with the exception of one company, on the eastern slope of the Green Mountains, and mustered into service while the battle of Bull Run was in progress. They were immediately sent to Washington, and since their arrival, during the last days of July, had been stationed at the Chain Bridge, some three miles above Georgetown. Company K, to which most of them belonged, was largely made up of farmer-boys, many of them still in their minority.

The story which I extracted from the "boys" was, in substance, this: William Scott, one of these mountain boys, just of age, had enlisted in Company K. Accustomed to his regular sound and healthy sleep, not yet inured to the life of the camp, he had volunteered to take the place of a sick comrade who had been detailed for picket duty, and had passed the night as a sentinel on guard. The next day he was himself detailed for the same duty, and undertook its performance. But he found it impossible to keep awake for two nights in succession, and had been found by the relief sound asleep on his post. For this offence he had been tried by a court-martial, found guilty, and sentenced to be shot within twenty-four hours after his trial, and on the second morning after his offence was committed.

Scott's comrades had set about saving him in a characteristic way. They had called a meeting, and appointed a committee, with power to use all the resources of the regiment in his behalf. Strangers in Washington, the committee had resolved to call on me for advice, because I was a Vermonter, and they had already marched from the camp to my office since daylight that morning.

The Captain took all the blame from Scott upon himself. Scott's mother opposed his enlistment on the ground of his inexperience, and had only consented on the Captain's promise to look after him as if he were his own son. This he had wholly failed to do. He must have been asleep or stupid himself, he said, when he paid no attention to the boy's statement that he had fallen asleep during the day, and feared he could not keep awake the second night on picket. Instead of sending some one or going himself in Scott's place, as he should, he had let him go to his death. He alone was guilty—"If any one ought to be shot, I am the fellow, and everybody at home would have the right to say so." "There must be some way to save him, judge!" (They all called me judge.) "He is as good a boy as there is in the army, and he ain't to blame. You will help us, now, won't you?" he said, almost with tears.

The other members of the committee had a definite, if not a practicable, plan. They insisted that Scott had not been tried, and gave this account of the proceeding. He was asked what he had to say to the charge, and said he would tell them just how it all happened. He had never been up all night that he remembered. He was "all beat out" by the night before, and knowing he should have a hard fight to keep awake, he thought of hiring one of the boys to go in his place, but they might think he was afraid to do his duty, and he decided to "chance it." Twice he went to sleep and woke himself while he was marching, and then—he could not tell anything about it—all he knew was that he was sound asleep when the guard came. It was very wrong, he knew. He wanted to be a good soldier, and do all his duty. What else did he enlist for? They could shoot him, and perhaps they ought to, but he could not have tried harder; and if he was in the same place again, he could no more help going to sleep than he could fly.

One must have been made of sterner stuff than I was not to be touched by the earnest manner with which these men offered to devote even their farms to the aid of their comrade. The Captain and the others had no need of words to express their emotions. I saw that the situation was surrounded by difficulties of which they knew nothing. They had subscribed a sum of money to pay counsel, and offered to pledge their credit to any amount necessary to secure him a fair trial.

"Put up your money," I said. "It will be long after this when one of my name takes money for helping a Vermont soldier. I know facts which touch this case of which you know nothing. I fear that nothing effectual can be done for your comrade. The courts and lawyers can do nothing. I fear that we can do no more; but we can try."

I must digress here to say that the Chain Bridge across the Potomac was one of the positions upon which the safety of Washington depended. The Confederates had fortified the approach to it on the Virginia side, and the Federals on the hills of Maryland opposite. Here, for months, the opposing forces had confronted each other. There had been no fighting; the men, and even the officers, had gradually contracted an intimacy, and, having nothing better to do, had swapped stories and other property until they had come to live upon the footing of good neighbors rather than mortal enemies. This relation was equally inconsistent with the safety of Washington and the stern discipline of war. Its discovery had excited alarm, and immediate measures were taken to break it up. General W. F. Smith, better known as "Baldy" Smith, had been appointed Colonel of the Third Vermont Regiment, placed in command of the post, and undertook to correct the irregularity.

General Smith, a Vermonter by birth, a West-Pointer by education, was a soldier from spur to crown. In the demoralization which existed at the Chain Bridge, in his opinion, the occasional execution of a soldier would tend to enforce discipline, and in the end promote economy of life. He had issued orders declaring the penalty of death for military offences, among others that of a sentinel sleeping upon his post. His orders were made to be obeyed. Scott was, apparently, their first victim. It was perfectly clear that any appeal in his behalf to General Smith would lead to nothing but loss of time.

The more I reflected upon what I was to do, the more hopeless the case appeared. Thought was useless; I must act upon impulse, or I should not act at all.

"Come," I said, "there is only one man on earth who can save your comrade. Fortunately, he is the best man on the continent. We will go to President Lincoln."

I went swiftly out of the Treasury over to the White House, and up the stairway to the little office where the President was writing. The boys followed in a procession. I did not give the thought time to get any hold on me that I, an officer of the government, was committing an impropriety in thus rushing a matter upon the President's attention. The President was the first to speak.

"What is this?" he asked. "An expedition to kidnap somebody, or to get another brigadier appointed, or for a furlough to go home to vote? I cannot do it, gentlemen. Brigadiers are thicker than drum-majors, and I couldn't get a furlough for myself if I asked it from the War Department."

There was hope in the tone in which he spoke. I went straight to my point. "Mr. President," I said, "these men want nothing for themselves. They are Green Mountain boys of the Third Vermont, who have come to stay as long as you need good soldiers. They don't want promotion until they earn it. But they do want something that you alone can give them—the life of a comrade."

"What has he done?" asked the President. "You Vermonters are not a bad lot, generally. Has he committed murder, or mutiny, or what other felony?"

"Tell him," I whispered to the Captain.

"I cannot! I cannot! I should stammer like a fool! You can do it better!"

"Captain," I said, pushing him forward, "Scott's life depends on you. You must tell the President the story. I know it only from hearsay."

He commenced like the man by the Sea of Galilee, who had an impediment in his speech; but very soon the string of his tongue was loosened, and he spoke plainly. As the words burst from his lips they stirred my own blood. He gave a graphic account of the whole story, and ended by saying, "He is as brave a boy as there is in your army, sir. Scott is no coward. Our mountains breed no cowards. They are the homes of thirty thousand men who voted for Abraham Lincoln. They will not be able to see that the best thing to be done with William Scott will be to shoot him like a traitor and bury him like a dog! Oh, Mr. Lincoln, can you?"

"No, I can't!" exclaimed the President. It was one of the moments when his countenance became such a remarkable study. It had become very earnest as the Captain rose with his subject; then it took on that melancholy expression which, later in his life, became so infinitely touching. I thought I could detect a mist in the deep cavities of his eyes. Then, in a flash, there was a total change. He smiled, and finally broke into a hearty laugh as he asked me:

"Do your Green Mountain boys fight as well as they talk? If they do, I don't wonder at the legends about Ethan Allen." Then his face softened as he said: "But what can I do? What do you expect me to do? As you know, I have not much influence with the departments?"

"I have not thought the matter out," I said. "I feel a deep interest in saving young Scott's life. I think I knew the boy's father. It is useless to apply to General Smith. An application to Secretary Stanton would only be referred to General Smith. The only thing to be done was to apply to you. It seems to me that, if you would sign an order suspending Scott's execution until his friends can have his case examined, I might carry it to the War Department, and so insure the delivery of the order to General Smith to-day, through the regular channels of the War Office."

"No! I do not think that course would be safe. You do not know these officers of the regular army. They are a law unto themselves. They sincerely think that it is a good policy occasionally to shoot a soldier. I can see it where a soldier deserts or commits a crime, but I cannot in such a case as Scott's. They say that I am always interfering with the discipline of the army and being cruel to the soldiers. Well, I can't help it, so I shall have to go right on doing wrong. I do not think an honest, brave soldier, conscious of no crime but sleeping when he was weary, ought to be shot or hung. The country has better uses for him.

"Captain," continued the President, "your boy shall not be shot—that is, not to-morrow, nor until I know more about his case." To me he said, "I will have to attend to this matter myself. I have for some time intended to go up to the Chain Bridge. I will do so to-day. I shall then know that there is no mistake in suspending the execution."

I remarked that he was undertaking a burden which we had no right to impose; that it was asking too much of the President in behalf of a private soldier.

"Scott's life is as valuable to him as that of any person in the land," he said. "You remember the remark of a Scotchman about the head of a nobleman who was decapitated. 'It was a small matter of a head, but it was valuable to him, poor fellow, for it was the only one he had.'"

I saw that remonstrance was vain. I suppressed the rising gratitude of the soldiers, and we took our leave. Two members of "the committee" remained to watch events in the city, while the others returned to carry the news of their success to Scott and to the camp. Later in the day the two members reported that the President had started in the direction of the camp; that their work here was ended, and they proposed to return to their quarters.

Within a day or two the newspapers reported that a soldier, sentenced to be shot for sleeping on his post, had been pardoned by the President and returned to his regiment. Other duties pressed me, and it was December before I heard anything further from Scott. Then another elderly soldier of the same company, whose health had failed and who was arranging for his own discharge, called upon me, and I made inquiry about Scott. The soldier gave an enthusiastic account of him. He was in splendid health, was very athletic, popular with everybody, and had the reputation of being the best all-around soldier in the company, if not in the regiment. His mate was the elderly soldier who had visited me with the party in September, who would be able to tell me all about him. To him I sent a message, asking him to see me when he was next in the city. His name was Ellis or Evans.

Not long afterwards he called at my office, and, as his leave permitted, I kept him overnight at my house, and gathered from him the following facts about Scott. He said that, as we supposed, the President went to the camp, and had a long conversation with Scott, at the end of which he was sent back to his company a free man. The President had given him a paper, which he preserved very carefully, which was supposed to be his discharge from the sentence. A regular order for his pardon had been read in the presence of the regiment, signed by General McClellan, but every one knew that his life had been saved by the President.

From that day Scott was the most industrious man in the company. He was always at work, generally helping some other soldier. His arms and his dress were neat and cleanly; he took charge of policing the company's quarters; was never absent at roll-call, unless he was sent away, and always on hand if there was any work to be done. He was very strong, and practised feats of strength until he could pick up a man lying on the ground and carry him away on his shoulders. He was of great use in the hospital, and in all the serious cases sought employment as a nurse, because it trained him in night-work and keeping awake at night. He soon attracted attention. He was offered promotion, which, for some reason, he declined.

It was a long time before he would speak of his interview with Mr. Lincoln. One night, when he had received a long letter from home, Scott opened his heart, and told Evans the story.

Scott said: "The President was the kindest man I had ever seen; I knew him at once by a Lincoln medal I had long worn. I was scared at first, for I had never before talked with a great man. But Mr. Lincoln was so easy with me, so gentle, that I soon forgot my fright. He asked me all about the people at home, the neighbors, the farm, and where I went to school, and who my schoolmates were. Then he asked me about mother, and how she looked, and I was glad I could take her photograph from my bosom and show it to him. He said how thankful I ought to be that my mother still lived, and how, if he was in my place, he would try to make her a proud mother, and never cause her a sorrow or a tear. I cannot remember it all, but every word was so kind.

"He had said nothing yet about that dreadful next morning. I thought it must be that he was so kind-hearted that he didn't like to speak of it. But why did he say so much about my mother, and my not causing her a sorrow or a tear when I knew that I must die the next morning? But I supposed that was something that would have to go unexplained, and so I determined to brace up and tell him that I did not feel a bit guilty, and ask him wouldn't he fix it so that the firing-party would not be from our regiment! That was going to be the hardest of all—to die by the hands of my comrades. Just as I was going to ask him this favor, he stood up, and he says to me, 'My boy, stand up here and look me in the face.' I did as he bade me. 'My boy,' he said, 'you are not going to be shot to-morrow. I believe you when you tell me that you could not keep awake. I am going to trust you, and send you back to your regiment. But I have been put to a good deal of trouble on your account. I have had to come up here from Washington when I have got a great deal to do; and what I want to know is, how are you going to pay my bill?' There was a big lump in my throat; I could scarcely speak. I had expected to die, you see, and had kind of got used to thinking that way. To have it all changed in a minute! But I got it crowded down, and managed to say, 'I am grateful, Mr. Lincoln! I hope I am as grateful as ever a man can be to you for saving my life. But it comes upon me sudden and unexpected like. I didn't lay out for it at all. But there is some way to pay you, and I will find it after a little. There is the bounty in the savings-bank. I guess we could borrow some money on the mortgage of the farm. There is my pay, and if you will wait until pay-day I am sure the boys will help, so I think we can make it up, if it isn't more than five or six hundred dollars,' 'But it is a great deal more than that,' he said. Then I said I didn't just see how, but I was sure I would find some way—if I lived.

"Then Mr. Lincoln put his hands on my shoulders and looked into my face as if he was sorry, and said: 'My boy, my bill is a very large one. Your friends cannot pay it, nor your bounty, nor the farm, nor all your comrades! There is only one man in all the world who can pay it, and his name is William Scott! If from this day William Scott does his duty, so that, if I were there when he comes to die, he could look me in the face as he does now, and say, I have kept my promise, and I have done my duty as a soldier, then my debt will be paid. Will you make that promise, and try to keep it?'

"I said I would make the promise, and, with God's help, I would keep it. I could not say any more. I wanted to tell him how hard I would try to do all he wanted; but the words would not come, so I had to let it all go unsaid. He went away, out of my sight forever. I know I shall never see him again; but may God forget me if I ever forget his kind words or my promise."

This was the end of the story of Evans, who got his discharge, and went home at the close of the year. I heard from Scott occasionally afterwards. He was gaining a wonderful reputation as an athlete. He was the strongest man in the regiment. The regiment was engaged in two or three reconnoissances in force, in which he performed the most exposed service with singular bravery. If any man was in trouble, Scott was his good Samaritan; if any soldier was sick, Scott was his nurse. He was ready to volunteer for any extra service or labor; he had done some difficult and useful scouting. He still refused promotion, saying that he had done nothing worthy of it. The final result was that he was the general favorite of all his comrades, the most popular man in the regiment, and modest, unassuming, and unspoiled by his success.

II

The next scene in this drama opens on the Peninsula, between the York and the James rivers, in March, 1862. The sluggish Warwick River runs from its source, near Yorktown, across the Peninsula to its discharge. It formed at that time a line of defence, which had been fortified by General Magruder, and was held by him with a force of some twelve thousand Confederates. Yorktown was an important position for the Confederates.

On the 15th of April the division of General Smith was ordered to stop the enemy's work on the entrenchments at Lee's Mills, the strongest position on the Warwick River. His force consisted of the Vermont brigade of five regiments, and three batteries of artillery. After a lively skirmish, which occupied the greater part of the forenoon, this order was executed, and should have ended the movement.

But about noon General McClellan with his staff, including the French princes, came upon the scene, and ordered General Smith to assault and capture the rebel works on the opposite bank. Some discretion was given to General Smith, who was directed not to bring on a general engagement, but to withdraw his men if he found the defence too strong to be overcome. This discretion cost many lives when the moment came for its exercise.

General Smith disposed his forces for the assault, which was made by Companies D, E, F, and K of the Third Vermont Regiment, covered by the artillery, with the Vermont Brigade in reserve. About four o'clock in the afternoon the charge was ordered. Unclasping their belts, and holding their guns and cartridge-boxes above their heads, the Vermonters dashed into and across the stream at Dam Number One, the strongest position in the

Confederate line, and cleared out the rifle-pits. But the earthworks were held by an overwhelming force of rebels, and proved impregnable. After a gallant attack upon the works the Vermonters were repulsed, and were ordered to retire across the river. They retreated under a heavy fire, leaving nearly half their number dead or wounded in the river and on the opposite shore.

Every member of these four companies was a brave man. But all the eye-witnesses agreed that among those who in this, their first hard battle, faced death without blenching, there was none braver or more efficient than William Scott, of Company K, debtor for his own life to President Lincoln. He was almost the first to reach the south bank of the river, the first in the rifle-pits, and the last to retreat. He recrossed the river with a wounded officer on his back; he carried him to a place of safety, and returned to assist his comrades, who did not agree on the number of wounded men saved by him from drowning or capture, but all agreed that he had carried the last wounded man from the south bank, and was nearly across the stream, when the fire of the rebels was concentrated upon him; he staggered with his living burden to the shore and fell.

An account of the closing scene in the life of William Scott was given me by a wounded comrade, as he lay upon his cot in a hospital tent, near Columbia College, in Washington, after the retreat of the army from the Peninsula. "He was all shot to pieces," said private H. "We carried him back, out of the line of fire, and laid him on the grass to die. His body was shot through and through, and the blood was pouring from his many wounds. But his strength was great, and such a powerful man was hard to kill. The surgeons checked the flow of blood—they said he had rallied from the shock; we laid him on a cot in a hospital tent, and the boys crowded around him, until the doctors said they must leave if he was to have any chance at all. We all knew he must die. We dropped on to the ground wherever we could, and fell into a broken slumber—wounded and well side by side. Just at daylight the word was passed that Scott wanted to see us all. We went into his tent and stood around his cot. His face was bright and his voice cheerful. 'Boys,' he said, 'I shall never see another battle. I supposed this would be my last. I haven't much to say. You all know what you can tell them at home about me. I have tried to do the right thing! I am almost certain you will all say that.' Then while his strength was failing, his life ebbing away, and we looked to see his voice sink into a whisper, his face lighted up and his voice came out natural and clear as he said: 'If any of you ever have the chance, I wish you would tell President Lincoln that I have never forgotten the kind words he said to me at the Chain Bridge—that I have tried to be a good soldier and true to the flag—that I should have paid my whole debt to him if I had lived; and that now, when I know that I am dying, I think of his kind face and thank him again, because he gave me the chance to fall like a soldier in battle, and not like a coward by the hands of my comrades.'

"His face, as he uttered these words, was that of a happy man. Not a groan or an expression of pain, not a word of complaint or regret from his lips. 'Good-bye, boys,' he said, cheerily. Then he closed his own eyes, crossed his hands on his breast, and—and—that was all. His face was at rest, and we all said it was beautiful. Strong men stood around his bed; they had seen their comrades fall, and had been very near to death themselves: such men are accustomed to control their feelings, but now they wept like children. One only spoke, as if to himself, 'Thank God, I know now how a brave man dies!'

"Scott would have been satisfied to rest in the same grave with his comrades," the wounded soldier continued. "But we wanted to know where he lay. There was a small grove of cherry-trees just in the rear of the camp, with a noble oak in its centre. At the foot of this oak we dug his grave. There we laid him, with his empty rifle and accoutrements by his side. Deep into the oak we cut the initials, W. S., and under it the words, 'A brave soldier.' Our chaplain said a short prayer. We fired a volley over his grave. Will you carry his last message to the President?" I answered, "Yes."

Some days passed before I again met the President. When I saw him I asked if he remembered William Scott?

"Of Company K, Third Vermont Volunteers?" he answered. "Certainly I do. He was the boy that Baldy Smith wanted to shoot at the Chain Bridge. What about William Scott?"

"He is dead. He was killed on the Peninsula," I answered. "I have a message from him for you, which I have promised one of his comrades to deliver."

A look of tenderness swept over his face as he exclaimed, "Poor boy! Poor boy! And so he is dead. And he sent me a message! Well, I think I will not have it now. I will come and see you."

He kept his promise. Before many days he made one of his welcome visits to my office. He said he had come to hear Scott's message. I gave it as nearly as possible in Scott's own words. Mr. Lincoln had perfect control of his own countenance; when he chose, he could make it a blank; when he did not care to control it, his was the most readable of speaking human faces. He drew out from me all I knew about Scott and about the people among whom he lived. When I spoke of the intensity of their sympathies, especially in sorrow and trouble, as a characteristic trait of mountaineers, he interrupted me and said, "It is equally common on the prairies. It is the privilege of the poor. I know all about it from experience, and I hope I have my full share of it. Yes, I can sympathize with sorrow."

"Mr. President," I said, "I have never ceased to reproach myself for thrusting Scott's case so unceremoniously before you—for causing you to take so much trouble for a private soldier. But I gave way to an impulse; I could not endure the thought that Scott should be shot. He was a fellow-Vermonter, and I knew there was no other way to save his life."

"I advise you always to yield to such impulses," he said. "You did me as great a favor as the boy. It was a new experience for me—a study that was interesting, though I have had more to do with people of his class than any other. Did you know that Scott and I had a long visit? I was much interested in the boy. I am truly sorry that he is dead, for he was a good boy—too good a boy to be shot for obeying nature. I am glad I interfered."

"Mr. Lincoln, I wish your treatment of this matter could be written into history."

"Tut, tut!" he broke in; "none of that. By-the-way, do you remember what Jeanie Deans said to Queen Caroline when the Duke of Argyle procured her an opportunity to beg for her sister's life?"

"I remember the incident well, but not the language."

"I remember both. This is the paragraph in point: 'It is not when we sleep soft and wake merrily ourselves that we think on other people's sufferings. Our hearts are waxed light within us then, and we are for righting our ain wrangs and fighting our ain battles. But when the hour of trouble comes to the mind or to the body—and when the hour of death comes, that comes to high and low—oh, then it isna what we hae dune for oursells, but what we hae dune for others, that we think on maist pleasantly. And the thoughts that ye hae intervened to spare the puir thing's life will be sweeter in that hour, come when it may, than if a word of your mouth could hang the whole Porteous mob at the tail of ae tow.'"

X

THE BATTLE BETWEEN THE "MONITOR" AND "MERRIMAC"

Told by Captain Worden and Lieutenant Greene of the "Monitor"

SOME weeks after the historic battle between the Monitor and the Merrimac in Hampton Roads, on March 9, 1862, the former vessel came to the Washington Navy-yard unchanged, in the same condition as when she discharged her parting shot at the Merrimac. There she lay until her heroic commander had so far recovered from his injuries as to be able to rejoin his vessel. All leaves of absence had been revoked, the absentees had returned, and were ready to welcome their Captain. President Lincoln, Captain Fox, and a limited number of Captain Worden's personal friends had been invited to his informal reception. Lieutenant Greene received the President and the guests. He was a boy in years—not too young to volunteer, however, when volunteers were scarce, and to fight the Merrimac during the last half of the battle, after the Captain was disabled.

The President and the other guests stood on the deck, near the turret. The men were formed in lines, with their officers a little in advance, when Captain Worden ascended the gangway. The heavy guns in the navy-yard began firing the customary salute when he stepped upon the deck. One side of his face was permanently blackened by the powder shot into it from the muzzle of a cannon carrying a shell of one hundred pounds' weight, discharged less than twenty yards away. The President advanced to welcome him, and introduced him to the few strangers present. The officers and men passed in review and were dismissed. Then there was a scene worth witnessing. The old tars swarmed around their loved captain, they grasped his hand, crowded to touch him, thanked God for his recovery and return, and invoked blessings upon his head in the name of all the saints in the calendar. He called them by their names, had a pleasant word for each of them, and for a few moments we looked upon an exhibition of a species of affection that could only have been the product of a common danger.

When order was restored, the President gave a brief sketch of Captain Worden's career. Commodore Paulding had been the first, Captain Worden the second officer of the navy, he said, to give an unqualified opinion in favor of armored vessels. Their opinions had been influential with him and with the Board of Construction. Captain Worden had volunteered to take command of the Monitor, at the risk of his life and reputation, before her keel was laid. He had watched her construction, and his energy had made it possible to send her to sea in time to arrest the destructive operations of the Merrimac. What he had done with a new crew, and a vessel of novel construction, we all knew. He, the President, cordially acknowledged his indebtedness to Captain Worden, and he hoped the whole country would unite in the feeling of obligation. The debt was a heavy one, and would not be repudiated when its nature was understood. The details of the first battle between iron-clads would interest every one. At the request of Captain Fox, Captain Worden had consented to give an account of his voyage from New York to Hampton Roads, and of what had afterwards happened there on board the Monitor.

In an easy, conversational manner, without any effort at display, Captain Worden told the story, of which the following is the substance:

"I suppose," he began, "that every one knows that we left New York Harbor in some haste. We had information that the Merrimac was nearly completed, and if we were to fight her on her first appearance, we must be on the ground. The Monitor had been hurried from the laying of her keel. Her engines were new, and her machinery did not move smoothly. Never was a vessel launched that so much needed trial-trips to test her machinery and get her crew accustomed to their novel duties. We went to sea practically without them. No part of the vessel was finished; there was one omission that was serious, and came very near causing her failure and the loss of many lives. In heavy weather it was intended that her hatches and all her openings should be closed and battened down. In that case all the men would be below, and would have to depend upon artificial ventilation. Our machinery for that purpose proved wholly inadequate.

"We were in a heavy gale of wind as soon as we passed Sandy Hook. The vessel behaved splendidly. The seas rolled over her, and we found her the most comfortable vessel we had ever seen, except for the ventilation, which gave us more trouble than I have time to tell you about. We had to run into port and anchor on account of the weather, and, as you know, it was two o'clock in the morning of Sunday before we were alongside the Minnesota. Captain Van Brunt gave us an account of Saturday's experience. He was very glad to make our acquaintance, and notified us that we must be prepared to receive the Merrimac at daylight. We had had a very hard trip down the coast, and officers and men were weary and sleepy. But when informed that our fight would probably open at daylight, and that the Monitor must be put in order, every man went to his post with a cheer. That night there was no sleep on board the Monitor.

"In the gray of the early morning we saw a vessel approaching, which our friends on the Minnesota said was the Merrimac. Our fastenings were cast off, our machinery started, and we moved out to meet her half-way. We had come a long way to fight her, and did not intend to lose our opportunity.

"Before showing you over the vessel, let me say that there were three possible points of weakness in the Monitor, two of which might have been guarded against in her construction, if there had been more time to perfect her plans. One of them was in the turret, which, as you see, is constructed of eight plates of inch iron—on the side of the ports, nine—set on end so as to break joints, and firmly bolted together, making a hollow cylinder eight inches thick. It rests on a metal ring on a vertical shaft, which is revolved by power from the boilers. If a projectile struck the turret at an acute angle, it was expected to glance off without doing damage. But what would happen if it was fired in a straight line to the centre of the turret, which in that case would receive the whole force of the blow? It might break off the bolt-heads on the interior, which, flying across, would kill the men at the guns; it might disarrange the revolving mechanism, and then we would be wholly disabled.

"I laid the Monitor close alongside the Merrimac, and gave her a shot. She returned our compliment by a shell, weighing one hundred and fifty pounds, fired when we were close together, which struck the turret so squarely that it received the whole force. Here you see the scar, two and a half inches deep in the wrought iron, a perfect mould of the shell. If anything could test the turret, it was that shot. It did not start a rivet-head or a nut! It stunned the two men who were nearest where the ball struck, and that was all. I touched the lever—the turret revolved as smoothly as before. The turret had stood the test; I could mark that point of weakness off my list forever.

"You notice that the deck is joined to the side of the hull by a right angle, at what sailors call the 'plank-shear.' If a projectile struck that angle, what would happen? It would not be deflected; its whole force would be expended there. It might open a seam in the hull below the water-line, or pierce the wooden hull, and sink us. Here was our second point of weakness.

"I had decided how I would fight her in advance. I would keep the Monitor moving in a circle, just large enough to give time for loading the guns. At the point where the circle impinged upon the Merrimac our guns should be fired, and loaded while we were moving around the circuit. Evidently the Merrimac would return the compliment every time. At our second exchange of shots, she returning six or eight to our two, another of her large shells struck our 'plank-shear' at its angle, and tore up one of the deck-plates, as you see. The shell had struck what I believed to be the weakest point in the Monitor. We had already learned that the Merrimac swarmed with sharp-shooters, for their bullets were constantly spattering against our turret and our deck. If a man showed himself on deck he would draw their fire. But I did not much consider the sharp-shooters. It was my duty to investigate the effects of that shot. I ordered one of the pendulums to be hauled aside, and, crawling out of the port, walked to the side, laid down upon my chest, and examined it thoroughly. The hull was uninjured, except for a few splinters in the wood. I walked back and crawled into the turret—the bullets were falling on the iron deck all about me as thick as hailstones in a storm. None struck me, I suppose because the vessel was moving, and at the angle, and when I was lying on the deck, my body made a small mark difficult to hit. We gave them two more guns, and then I told the men, what was true, that the Merrimac could not sink us if we let her pound us for a month. The men cheered; the knowledge put new life into all.

"We had more exchanges, and then the Merrimac tried new tactics. She endeavored to ram us, to run us down. Once she struck us about amidships with her iron ram. Here you see its mark. It gave us a shock, pushed us around, and that was all the harm. But the movement placed our sides together. I gave her two guns, which I think lodged in her side, for, from my lookout crack, I could not see that either shot rebounded. Ours being the smaller vessel, and more easily handled, I had no difficulty in avoiding her ram. I ran around her several times, planting our shot in what seemed to be the most vulnerable places. In this way, reserving my fire until I got the range and the mark, I planted two more shots almost in the very spot I had hit when she tried to ram us. Those shots must have been effective, for they were followed by a shower of bars of iron.

"The third weak spot was our pilot-house. You see that it is built a little more than three feet above the deck, of bars of iron, ten by twelve inches square, built up like a log-house, bolted with very large bolts at the corners where the bars interlock. The pilot stands upon a platform below, his head and shoulders in the pilot-house. The upper tier of bars is separated from the second by an open space of an inch, through which the pilot may look out at every point of the compass. The pilot-house, as you see, is a four-square mass of iron, provided with no means of deflecting a ball. I expected trouble from it, and I was not disappointed. Until my accident happened, as we approached the enemy I stood in the pilot-house and gave the signals. Lieutenant Greene fired the guns, and Engineer Stimers, here, revolved the turret.

"I was below the deck when the corner of the pilot-house was first struck by a shot or a shell. It either burst or was broken, and no harm was done. A short time after I had given the signal, and with my eye close against the lookout crack, was watching the effect of our shot, when something happened to me—my part in the fight was ended. Lieutenant Greene, who fought the Merrimac until she had no longer stomach for fighting, will tell you the rest of the story."

Can it be possible that this beardless boy fought one of the historic battles of the world? This was the thought of every one, as the modest, diffident young Greene was half pushed forward into the circle.

THE BATTLE BETWEEN THE "MONITOR" AND "MERRIMAC"

"I cannot add much to the Captain's story," he began. "He had cut out the work for us, and we had only to follow his pattern. I kept the Monitor either moving around the circle or around the enemy, and endeavored to place our shots as near her amidships as possible, where Captain Worden believed he had already broken through her armor. We knew that she could not sink us, and I thought I would keep right on pounding her as long as she would stand it. There is really nothing new to be added to Captain Worden's account. We could strike her wherever we chose; weary as they must have been, our men were full of enthusiasm, and I do not think we wasted a shot. Once we ran out of the circle for a moment to adjust a piece of machinery, and I learn that some of our friends feared that we were drawing out of the fight. The Merrimac took the opportunity to start for Norfolk. As soon as our machinery was adjusted we followed her, and got near enough to give her a parting shot. But I was not familiar with the locality; there might be torpedoes planted in the channel, and I did not wish to take any risk of losing our vessel, so I came back to the company of our friends. But except that we were, all of us, tired and hungry when we came back to the Minnesota at half-past twelve P.M., the Monitor was just as well prepared to fight as she was at eight o'clock in the morning when she fired the first gun."

We were then shown the injury to the pilot-house. The mark of the ball was plain upon the two upper bars, the principal impact being upon the lower of the two. This huge bar was broken in the middle, but held firmly at either end. The further it was pressed in, the stronger was the resistance on the exterior. On the inside the fracture in the bar was half an inch wide. Captain Worden's eye was very near to the lookout crack, so that when the gun was discharged the shock of the ball knocked him senseless, while the mass of flame filled one side of his face with coarse grains of powder. He remained insensible for some hours.

"Have you heard what Captain Worden's first inquiry was when he recovered his senses after the general shock to his system?" asked Captain Fox of the President.

"I think I have," replied Mr. Lincoln, "but it is worth relating to these gentlemen."

"His question was," said Captain Fox, "'Have I saved the Minnesota?'

"'Yes, and whipped the Merrimac!' some one answered."

"'Then,' said Captain Worden, 'I don't care what becomes of me.'"

"Mr. President," said Captain Fox, "not much of the history to which we have listened is new to me. I saw this battle from eight o'clock until midday. There was one marvel in it which has not been mentioned—the splendid handling of the Monitor throughout the battle. The first bold advance of this diminutive vessel against a giant like the Merrimac was superlatively grand. She seemed inspired by Nelson's order at Trafalgar: 'He will make no mistake who lays his vessel alongside the enemy.' One would have thought the Monitor a living thing. No man was visible. You saw her moving around that circle, delivering her fire invariably at the point of contact, and heard the crash of the missile against her enemy's armor above the thunder of her guns, on the bank where we stood. It was indescribably grand!

"Now," he continued, "standing here on the deck of this battle-scarred vessel, the first genuine iron-clad—the victor in the first fight of iron-clads—let me make a confession, and perform an act of simple justice. I never fully believed in armored vessels until I saw this battle. I know all the facts which united to give us the Monitor. I withhold no credit from Captain Ericsson, her inventor, but I know that the country is principally indebted for the construction of this vessel to President Lincoln, and for the success of her trial to Captain Worden, her commander."

XI
SHERIDAN'S RIDE

Told by his Aide

"When I heard this I took two of my aides-de-camp, Major George A. Forsyth and Captain Joseph O'Keeffe, and with twenty men from the escort started for the front."—From the Personal Memoirs of P. H. Sheridan, vol. ii., chap, iii., page 80.

IN the summer of 1864 I was on detached duty as an acting aide on the staff of Major-General Philip H. Sheridan, then in command of the Army of the Shenandoah. I was one of two officers who rode to the front with him "from Winchester down" on October 19, 1864, the day of the battle of Cedar Creek.

It seemed as though the campaign in the valley of the Shenandoah in the year 1864 was practically over. Twice within four days General Sheridan had attacked and defeated the Confederate army under General Early: first, on September 19th, at the crossing of Opequon Creek, in front of Winchester, Virginia, and again at Fisher's Hill, twenty-two miles farther up the valley, on the twenty-second day of the same month. Both victories had been wrung from the enemy by dint of hard fighting and good judgment on the part of the commanding general of the United States forces, and his reputation as the commander of an army was now seemingly as secure as the brilliant record he had already made as a brigade, division, and corps commander.

The Federal troops lay quietly in camp in fancied security near Strasburg, just in rear of Cedar Creek, one of the tributaries of the Shenandoah River, and the shattered forces of the enemy were supposed to be somewhere in the vicinity of Gordonsville, Virginia; but the Confederate general, Jubal A. Early, was a soldier unused to defeat, a bitter enemy and a desperate foe, and as later events went to show, an officer willing to risk his all on the mere possibility of regaining, by a sudden and unexpected blow, the lost prestige of himself and army. In my opinion, but for the opportune arrival of General Sheridan on the field of battle, there is no reasonable doubt that he would have succeeded in accomplishing his object.

On the morning of October 19th, about daylight, word was brought from the picket-line south of Winchester of heavy firing at the front. General Sheridan interviewed the officer who brought the information, and decided that it must be the result of the reconnoissance that General Wright had notified him the night before was to take place this morning. Little apprehension was occasioned by the report. After breakfast, probably nearly or quite nine o'clock, we mounted and rode at a walk through the town of Winchester to Mill Creek, a mile south of the village, where we found our escort awaiting us.

We could occasionally hear the far-away sound of heavy guns, and as we moved out with our escort behind us I thought that the General was becoming anxious. He leaned forward and listened intently, and once he dismounted and placed his ear near the ground, seeming somewhat disconcerted as he rose again and remounted. We had not gone far, probably not more than a mile, when, at the crest of a little hill on the road, we found the pike obstructed by some supply-trains which had started on their way to the army. They were now halted, and seemingly in great confusion. Part of the wagons faced one way, part the other; others were half turned round, in position to swing either way, but were huddled together, completely blocking the road.

Turning to me, the General said, "Ride forward quickly and find out the trouble here, and report promptly." I rode rapidly to the head of the train and asked for the quartermaster in charge, and was told he had gone up the road a short distance.

On reaching him, I found him conversing with a quartermaster-sergeant. They informed me that an officer had come from the front and told them to go back at once, as our army had been attacked at daylight, defeated, and was being driven down the valley. The officer, they said, had gone back towards the front after warning them to come no farther.

Galloping back, I made my report. "Pick out fifty of the best-mounted men from the escort," was the response. Riding down the column, with the aid of one of the officers of the regiment, this was soon accomplished, and I reported with the selected men. Turning to his chief of staff, Colonel J. W. Forsyth, the General said something regarding certain instructions he had evidently been giving him, and then said to me, "You and Captain O'Keeffe will go with me;" and nodding good-bye to the other gentlemen of our party, with whom he had probably been conferring while I was making up the cavalry detail, he turned his horse's head southward, tightening the reins of his bridle, and with a slight touch of the spur he dashed up the turnpike and was off. A yard in rear, and side by side, Captain O'Keeffe and myself swept after him, while the escort, breaking from a trot to a gallop, came thundering on behind.

The distance from Winchester to Cedar Creek, on the north bank of which the Army of the Shenandoah lay encamped, is a little less than nineteen miles. The general direction was west of south, and the road to it, by way of the valley pike, ran directly through the road-side hamlets of Milltown, Kearnstown, Newtown, and Middletown. Our army was encamped four miles south of Middletown. The Shenandoah Valley turnpike, over which we were now speeding, was formerly a well-built macadamized road, laid in crushed limestone, and until the advent of the war had been kept in excellent condition. Even then, though worn for three years past by the tread of contending armies with all the paraphernalia of war as they swept up and down the valley, it was a fairly good road; but the army supply-trains, ammunition-wagons, and artillery had worn it into deep ruts in places, and everywhere the dust lay thick and heavy on its surface, and powdered the trees and bushes that fringed its sides, so that our galloping column sent a gray cloud swirling behind us. It was a golden sunny day that had succeeded a densely foggy October morning. The turnpike stretched away, a white, dusty line, over hill and through dale, bordered by fenceless fields, and past farm-houses and empty barns and straggling orchards. Now and then it ran through a woody copse, with here and there a tiny stream of water crossing it, or meandering by its side, so clear and limpid that it seemed to invite us to pause and slake our thirst as we sped along our dusty way. On either side we saw, through the Indian-summer haze, the distant hills covered with woods and fairly ablaze with foliage; and over all was the deep blue of a cloudless southern sky, making it a day on which one's blood ran riot and he was glad of health and life.

Within a mile we met more supply-trains that had turned back, and the General stopped long enough to order the officer in charge to halt, park his trains just where he was, and await further instructions. Then on we dashed again, only to meet, within a few moments, more supply-trains hurrying to the rear. The General did not stop, but signalling the officer in charge to join him, gave him instructions on the gallop to park his train at once, and use his escort to arrest and stop all stragglers coming from the army, and to send back to the front all well men who might drift to him, under guard if necessary.

Scarcely had we parted from him and surmounted the next rise in the road when we came suddenly upon indubitable evidence of battle and retreat. About a mile in advance of us the road was filled and the fields dotted with wagons and men belonging to the various brigade, division, and corps headquarters, and in among them officers' servants with led horses, and here and there a broken ambulance, sutlers' supply-trains, a battery forge or two, horses and mules hastily packed with officers' mess-kits, led by their cooks, and now and then a group of soldiers, evidently detailed enlisted men attached to the headquarters trains. In fact, this was the first driftwood of a flood just beyond and soon to come sweeping down the road. Passing this accumulation of débris with a rush by leaving the pike and galloping over the open fields on the side of the road, we pushed rapidly on; but not so quickly but that we caught an echoing cheer from the enlisted men and servants, who recognized the General, and shouted and swung their hats in glee.

Within the next few miles the pike and adjacent fields began to be lined and dotted everywhere with army wagons, sutlers' outfits, headquarters supply-trains, disabled caissons, and teamsters with led mules, all drifting to the rear; and now and then a wounded officer or enlisted man on horseback or plodding along on foot, with groups of straggling soldiers here and there among the wagon-trains, or in the fields, or sometimes sitting or lying down to rest by the side of the road, while others were making coffee in their tin cups by tiny camp-fires. Soon we began to see small bodies of soldiers in the fields with stacked arms, evidently cooking breakfast. As we turned into the fields and passed around the wagons and through these groups, the General would wave his hat to the men and point to the front, never lessening his speed as he pressed forward. It was enough; one glance at the eager face and familiar black horse and they knew him, and starting to their feet, they swung their caps around their heads and broke into cheers as he passed beyond them; and then, gathering up their belongings and shouldering their arms, they started after him for the front, shouting to their comrades farther out in the fields, "Sheridan! Sheridan!" waving their hats, and pointing after him as he dashed onward; and they too comprehended instantly, for they took up the cheer and turned back for the battlefield.

To the best of my recollection, from the time we met the first stragglers who had drifted back from the army, his appearance and his cheery shout of "Turn back, men! turn back! Face the other way!" as he waved his hat towards the front, had but one result: a wild cheer of recognition, an answering wave of the cap. In no case, as I glanced back, did I fail to see the men shoulder their arms and follow us. I think it is no exaggeration to say that as he dashed on to the field of battle, for miles back the turnpike was lined with men pressing forward after him to the front.

So rapid had been our gait that nearly all of the escort, save the commanding officer and a few of his best-mounted men, had been distanced, for they were more heavily weighted, and ordinary troop horses could not live at such a pace. Once we were safe among our own people, their commander had the good sense to see that his services were no longer a necessity, and accordingly drew rein and saved his horses by following on at a slow trot. Once the General halted a moment to speak to an officer he knew and inquire for information. As he did so he turned and asked me to get him a switch; for he usually rode carrying a light riding-whip, and furthermore he had broken one of the rowels of his spurs. Dismounting, I cut one from a near-by way-side bush, hastily trimmed it, and gave it him. "Thanks, Sandy," said he, and as we started again he struck his splendid black charger Rienzi a slight blow across the shoulder with it, and he at once broke into that long swinging gallop, almost a run, which he seemed to maintain so easily and so endlessly—a most distressing gait for those who had to follow far. These two words of thanks were almost the only ones he addressed to me until we reached the army; but my eyes had sought his face at every opportunity, and my heart beat high with hope from what I saw there. As he galloped on his features gradually grew set, as though carved in stone, and the same dull red glint I had seen in his piercing black eyes when, on other occasions, the battle was going against us, was there now. Occasionally Captain O'Keeffe and myself exchanged a few words, and we waved our hats and shouted to the men on the road and in the fields as we passed them, pointing to the General and seconding as best we could his energetic shout: "Turn back, men! turn back! Face the other way!" Now and then I would glance at the face of my companion, Captain O'Keeffe, whose gray-blue eyes fairly danced with excitement at the prospect of the coming fray; for if ever a man was a born soldier and loved fighting for chivalry's sake, it was that gallant young Irish gentleman, Joe O'Keeffe.

Each moment that we advanced the road became more closely clogged with stragglers and wounded men, and here the General suddenly paused to speak to one of the wounded officers, from whom I judge he got his only correct idea of the attack by the enemy at dawn, the crushing of our left, and the steady outflanking that had forced our army back to where it was at present, for I caught something of what the officer said, and his ideas seemed to be clear and concise. This pause was a piece of rare good-fortune for me, for my orderly happened to be by the side of the road with my led horse, and in a trice he changed my saddle, and I rejoined the General ere he was a hundred yards away, with all the elation that a fresh mount after a weary one inspires in the heart of a cavalryman.

Within a comparatively short distance we came suddenly upon a field-hospital in a farm-house close to the road beyond Newtown, where the medical director had established part of his corps. Just ahead of us the road was filled with ambulances containing wounded men, who were being carried into the house to be operated upon, while outside of the door along the foot-path lay several dead men, who had been hastily placed there on being taken from the stretchers.

In our immediate front the road and adjacent fields were filled with sections of artillery, caissons, ammunition-trains, ambulances, battery-wagons, squads of mounted men, led horses, wounded soldiers, broken wagons, stragglers, and stretcher-bearers—in fact, all that appertains to and is part of the rear of an army in action. One hasty glance as we galloped forward and we had taken in the situation. About half or three-quarters of a mile this side of Middletown, with its left resting upon the turnpike, was a division of infantry in line of battle at right angles to the road, with its standards flying, and evidently held well in hand. Near the turnpike, and just to its left, one of our batteries was having a savage artillery duel with a Confederate battery, which was in position on a little hill to the left and rear of Middletown as we faced it. To the left of this battery of ours were the led horses of a small brigade of cavalry, which was holding the ground to the left of the pike, and both the infantry and cavalry dismounted skirmishers were in action with those of the enemy. Farther to the left, and slightly to the rear, on a bit of rising ground, was another of our batteries in action. Half a mile to the right, and somewhat to the rear of the division of infantry which was in line of battle, could be seen a body of infantry in column slowly retiring and tending towards the pike; and just beyond these troops was another body of infantry, also in column, and also moving in the same general direction. Farther to the right, across a small valley, and more than a mile away from these last-mentioned troops, was a still larger force of infantry, on a side-hill, facing towards the enemy, in line of battle, but not in action. I looked in vain for the cavalry divisions, but concluded rightly that they were somewhere on the flanks of the enemy.

"SHERIDAN! SHERIDAN!"

Skirting the road, and avoiding as best we might the impediments of battle, the General, O'Keeffe, and myself spurred forward. Finally, on the open road and just before we reached the troops in line, which was Getty's division of the Sixth Army Corps, I asked permission to go directly down to the skirmish-line to see the actual condition of things. "Do so," replied the General, "and report as soon as possible." Just then we reached the line, and as I glanced back I saw the chief draw rein in the midst of the division, where he was greeted by a storm of cheers and wild cries of "Sheridan! Sheridan!" while standards seemed to spring up out of the very earth to greet him.

I rode rapidly back to my chief, whom I found dismounted, surrounded by several general officers, and in the midst of those of his staff who had not gone with us to Washington. Dismounting, I saluted. Stepping on one side from the group, he faced me, and said,

"Well?"

"You see where we are?" (A nod.) "Lowell says that our losses, killed, wounded, and missing, are between three and five thousand, and more than twenty guns, to say nothing of transportation. He thinks he can hold on where he is for forty minutes longer, possibly sixty."

I can see him before me now as I write, erect, looking intently in my eyes, his left hand resting, clinched savagely, on the top of the hilt of his sabre, his right nervously stroking his chin, his eyes with that strange red gleam in them, and his attenuated features set as if cast in bronze. He stood mute and absolutely still for more than ten seconds; then, throwing up his head, he said:

"Go to the right and find the other two divisions of the Sixth Corps and also General Emory's command [the two divisions of the Nineteenth Corps]. Bring them up, and order them to take position on the right of Getty. Lose no time." And as I turned to mount, he called out: "Stay! I'll go with you!" And springing on his horse, we set off together, followed by the staff.

In a few moments we had reached the head of the nearest division we were seeking. It was ordered on the line—I think by the General himself; and as I started for the head of the other division, he ordered me to ride directly over to General Emory's command (two divisions of the Nineteenth Corps), and order it up, to take position in line of battle on the right of the Sixth Corps. I rode over to General Emory's line, which was about a mile away, and found his troops in good condition, though somewhat shattered by the fortunes of the day, facing towards the enemy, and half covered by small ledges of rock that cropped out of the hill-side. On receiving the order, he called my attention to the fact that in case the enemy advanced on the Sixth Corps, he would be nearly on their flank, and he thought best that I tell the commanding general of the fact, as it might induce him to modify the order. Galloping back, I gave his suggestion to the General.

"No, no!" he replied. "Get him over at once—at once! Don't lose a moment!"

I fairly tore back, and the troops were promptly put in motion for their new position, which they reached in due time, and were formed in line of battle in accordance with General Sheridan's orders.

After the whole line was thoroughly formed, I rode over to my chief and urged him to ride down it, that all the men might see him, and know without doubt that he had returned and assumed command. At first he demurred, but I was most urgent, as I knew that in some instances both men and officers who had not seen him doubted his arrival. His appearance was greeted by tremendous cheers from one end of the line to the other, many of the officers pressing forward to shake his hand. He spoke to them all, cheerily and confidently, saying: "We are going back to our camps, men, never fear. I'll get a twist on these people yet. We'll raise them out of their boots before the day is over."

At no time did I hear him utter that "terrible oath" so often alluded to in both prose and poetry in connection with this day's work.

As we turned to go back from the end of the line, he halted on the line of the Nineteenth Corps and said to me: "Stay here and help fight this corps. I will send orders to General Emory through you. Give orders in my name, if necessary. Stay right on this line with it."

"Very good, General," was my reply; and the General and staff left me there and galloped towards the pike.

It must have been nearly or quite half-past twelve o'clock by this time, and as soon as the skirmishers were thrown forward the troops were ordered to lie down: an order gladly obeyed, for they had been on their feet since daylight, fighting and without food. They were to have but a short period of rest, however, for in a few moments the low rustling murmur, that presages the advance of a line of battle through dense woods (the Nineteenth Corps was formed just at the outer edge of a belt of heavy timber) began to make itself felt, and in a moment the men were in line again. A pattering fire in front, and our skirmishers came quickly back through the woods, and were absorbed in the line; then there was a momentary lull, followed by a rustling, crunching sound as the enemy's line pressed forward, trampling the bushes under-foot and crowding through bits of underbrush.

In a flash we caught a glimpse of a long, gray line stretching away through the woods on either side of us, advancing with waving standards, with here and there a mounted officer in rear of it. At the same instant the dark-blue line at the edge of the woods seemed to burst upon their view, for suddenly they halted, and with a piercing yell poured in a heavy volley, that was almost instantly answered from our side, and then volleys seemed fairly to leap from one end to the other of our line, and a steady roar of musketry from both sides made the woods echo again in every direction. Gradually, however, the sounds became less heavy and intense, the volleys slowly died away, and we began to recognize the fact that the enemy's bullets were no longer clipping the twigs above us, and that their fire had about ceased, while a ringing cheer along our front proclaimed that for the first time that day the Confederate army had been repulsed.

During the attack my whole thought, and I believe that of every officer on the line, had been to prevent our troops from giving way. In one or two places the line wavered slightly, but the universal shout of, "Steady, men, steady, steady!" as the field-officers rode up and down the line, seemed to be all that was needed to inspire the few nervous ones with renewed courage and hold them well up to their work. As for myself, I was more than satisfied, for only years of personal experience in war enable a man to appreciate at its actual value the tremendous gain when a routed army turns, faces, and checks a triumphant enemy in the open field. It is a great thing to do it with the aid of reinforcements; it is a glorious thing to do it without.

For a few moments the men stood leaning on their arms, and some of us mounted officers rode slowly forward, anxiously peering through the trees, but save for a dead man or two there was no sign of the enemy; the Confederates had fallen back. Word was passed back to the line, and the men were ordered to lie down, which they willingly did.

After a time the news ran down the line that we were to advance. Springing to their feet at the word of command, the tired troops stood to arms and seemed to resolutely shake off the depression that had sat so heavily upon them, and began to pull themselves together for the coming fray. Everywhere along the line of battle men might be seen to stoop and retie their shoes; to pull their trousers at the ankle tightly together and then draw up their heavy woollen stockings over them; to rebuckle and tighten their waist-belts; to unbutton the lids of their cartridge-boxes and pull them forward rather more to the front; to rearrange their haversacks and canteens, and to shift their rolls of blankets in order to give freer scope to the expansion of their shoulders and an easier play to their arms; to set their forage-caps tighter on their heads, pulling the visor well down over their eyes; and then, almost as if by order, there rang from one end of the line to the other the rattle of ramrods and snapping of gunlocks as each man tested for himself the condition of his rifle, and made sure that his weapon was in good order and to be depended upon in the emergency that was so soon to arise. Then, grounding arms, they stood at ease, half leaning on their rifles, saying little, but quietly awaiting orders and grimly gazing straight towards the front. In front of the battalions, with drawn swords and set lips, stood their line-officers, slightly craning their heads forward and looking into the woods, as if trying to catch a glimpse of the enemy they knew to be somewhere there, but whom as yet they could not see.

I push through the line slightly forward of the nearest brigade, and in a moment the sharp command, "Attention!" rings down the line. "Shoulder arms! Forward! March!" And with martial tread and floating flags the line of battle is away. "Guide left!" shout the line-officers. "Guide left—left!" and that is the only order I hear as we press forward through the thick trees and underbrush. I lean well forward on my horse's neck, striving to catch if possible a glimpse of the Confederate line; but hark! Here comes the first shot. "Steady! Steady, men!" Another, and now a few scattering bullets come singing through the woods. The line does not halt or return the fire, but presses steadily on to the oft-repeated command of "Forward! forward!" that never ceases to ring from one end to the other of the advancing line. Soon the woods become less dense, and through the trees I see just beyond us an open field partly covered with small bushes, and several hundred yards away, crowning a slight crest on its farther side, a low line of fence-rails and loose stones, which, as we leave the edge of the woods, and come into the open, suddenly vomits flame and smoke along its entire length, and a crashing volley tells us that we have found the enemy. For an instant our line staggers, but the volley has been aimed too high and few men fall. "Steady—steady, men!" shout the officers. "Aim!" and almost instinctively the whole line throw forward their pieces. "Fire!" and the next instant a savage volley answers that of the Confederates. I can see that it has told, too, for in several places along the opposite crest men spring to their feet as if to fall back, but their officers promptly rally them. "Pour it into them, men!" shout our officers. "Let them have it. It's our turn now!" for brute instinct has triumphed and the savage is uppermost with all of us. For a moment or two the men stand and fire at will, as rapidly as it is possible to reload, and then the Confederate fire seems to slowly slacken; so, with a universal shout of "Forward! forward!" we press towards the enemy's line. Before we are much more than half-way across the field, however, they seem to have abandoned our front, for I cannot see anything ahead of us, though I stand up in my stirrups and look eagerly forward. But what—what is that? Crash! crash! and from a little bush-covered plateau on our right the enemy sends a couple of rattling volleys on our exposed flank that do us great harm, and I realize that we are the outflanked!

For an instant the line gives way, but every mounted officer in the vicinity, among whom I recognize General Fessenden, seems to be instantly on the spot trying to rally the troops and hold the line. "Steady! steady! Right wheel!" is the shout, and the men, after the first flush of surprise, behave splendidly, one young color-bearer rushing to the right and waving his flag defiantly in the new direction from which the enemy's fire is now coming. I ask him to let me take it, as I am mounted and it can be seen better, as there is some undergrowth at this particular spot in the field. At first he demurs, but seeing the point, yields. Holding on to my saddle, the color-bearer accompanies me towards a slight hillock. The line catches sight of it, and the left begins to swing slowly round, the men in our immediate vicinity loading and firing as rapidly as they can in the direction from which the enemy is now advancing. The Confederates are giving it to us hotly, and we realize that we have lost the continuity of our line on both flanks.

Suddenly peal on peal of musketry broke out on our right, and the copse in front of us was fairly bullet-swept by repeated volleys. The next moment a portion of one of McMillan's brigades, which he had promptly swung round and faced to the right, dashed forward, and together we moved up to the position just held by the enemy, to find that he was in headlong retreat. One hasty look, and I saw that we had pierced the enemy's line, and that his extreme left was cut off and scattered. But I could not see any troops nor anything of his line over in the direction of the pike, as there was a dense belt of woods that shut out the view. Nevertheless, the steady roar of artillery and peals of musketry told us that heavy fighting was going on in that part of the field. General McMillan was already re-forming his men to move over and take up the line and our former direction to the left, when General Sheridan, riding his gray charger Breckenridge, and surrounded by his staff, came out of the woods and dashed up. One glance and he had the situation. "This is all right! this is all right!" was his sole comment. Then turning to General McMillan, he directed him to continue the movement and close up to the left and complete our line of battle as it originally was.

He told me, however, to hold the troops until I saw that Custer had driven the enemy's cavalry from our flank. This we could easily see, as the country was open and the ground lower than where we were. Having given these instructions, the General, followed by his staff, galloped rapidly to the left and rear through the woods, evidently making for the pike, where, judging from the continued roar of field-guns and musketry the Sixth Corps was having savage work.

As soon as we saw General Custer's squadrons charge across the field and engage the enemy's cavalry, General McMillan ordered the advance, and we pushed forward, driving the enemy ahead of us through the wood, and came out to the left and rear of the Confederate line, enabling our left to pour in a fearful fire on their exposed flank. The enemy was gallantly holding his line behind some stone fences, but "flesh that is born of woman" could not stand such work as this, and the cavalry, having got well in on their right flank about this time, their entire line gave way in retreat.

Our whole army now pressed rapidly forward, not stopping to re-form, but driving them from each new line of defence; yet it was no walk-over even then, for the Confederates fought splendidly—desperately even. They tried to take advantage of every stone fence, house, or piece of woods on which to rally their men and retard our advance. Their batteries were served gallantly and handled brilliantly, and took up position after position; but it was all in vain, for we outnumbered them, both cavalry and infantry, and their men must have comprehended the fact that our cavalry was turning both their flanks.

For a few moments the Confederates held their position on the hills, but suddenly abandoned it in haste and sought safety in flight, for some of General Custer's cavalry had crossed the creek at the ford below and were getting in their rear, and to remain was to be captured. I soon caught up with some of our cavalry regiments, and we started in full cry after the enemy. It was no use for them to attempt anything but flight from this on, and they abandoned everything and got away from our pursuing squadrons as best they might, hundreds of them leaving the pike and scattering through the hills. The road was literally crammed with abandoned wagons, ambulances, caissons, and artillery.

At a small bridge, where a creek crosses the road some distance south of the town, we were fired upon from the opposite side by what I thought was the last organized force of General Early's army. I now believe it to have been his provost guard with a large body of our prisoners captured by the enemy early in the day. The planks of this bridge were torn up to prevent the enemy from coming back during the night and carrying off any of the captured property. I then started to return to headquarters, counting the captured cannon as I went. It soon occurred to me that it was so dark I might mistake a caisson for a gun, so I dismounted and placed my hand on each piece. I reached headquarters about half-past eight or possibly nine o'clock. Camp-fires were blazing everywhere. I went up to the chief, who was standing near a bright fire surrounded by a group of officers, and saluted, reporting my return.

"Where do you come from?"

"Beyond Strasburg."

"What news have you?"

"The road is lined with transportation of almost every kind, and we have captured forty-four pieces of artillery."

"How do you know that we have forty-four pieces?"

"I have placed my hand on each and every gun."

Standing there in the firelight I saw my chief's face light up with a great wave of satisfaction.

XII
LEE'S SURRENDER AT APPOMATTOX

Told by One Who was Present

WHEN, on the night of the 8th of April, 1865, the cavalry corps of the Army of the Potomac reached the two or three little houses that made up the settlement at Appomattox Depot—the station on the South-side Railroad that connects Appomattox Court-house with the travelling world—it must have been nearly or quite dark. At about nine o'clock or half-past, while standing near the door of one of the houses, it occurred to me that it might be well to try and get a clearer idea of our immediate surroundings, as it was not impossible that we might have hot work here or near here before the next day fairly dawned upon us.

My "striker" had just left me with instructions to have my horse fed, groomed, and saddled before daylight. As he turned to go he paused and put this question: "Do you think, Colonel, that we'll get General Lee's army to-morrow?"

"I don't know," was my reply; "but we will have some savage fighting if we don't."

As the sturdy young soldier said "Good-night, sir," and walked away, I knew that if the enlisted men of our army could forecast the coming of the end so plainly, there was little hope of the escape of the Army of Northern Virginia.

I walked up the road a short distance, and looked carefully about me to take my bearings. It was a mild spring night, with a cloudy sky, and the soft mellow smell of earthiness in the atmosphere that not infrequently portends rain. If rain came then it might retard the arrival of our infantry, which I knew General Sheridan was most anxious should reach us at the earliest possible moment. A short distance from where I stood was the encampment of our headquarters escort, with its orderlies, grooms, officers' servants, and horses. Just beyond it could be seen the dying camp-fires of a cavalry regiment, lying close in to cavalry corps headquarters. This regiment was in charge of between six and eight hundred prisoners, who had fallen into our hands just at dark, as Generals Custer and Devin, at the head of their respective cavalry commands, had charged into the station and captured four railway trains of commissariat supplies, which had been sent here to await the arrival of the Confederate army, together with twenty-six pieces of artillery. For a few moments the artillery had greatly surprised and astonished us, for its presence was entirely unexpected, and as it suddenly opened on the charging columns of cavalry it looked for a short time as though we might have all unwittingly fallen upon a division of infantry. However, it turned out otherwise. Our cavalry, after the first recoil, boldly charged in among the batteries, and the gunners, being without adequate support, sensibly surrendered. The whole affair was for us a most gratifying termination of a long day's ride, as it must have proved later on a bitter disappointment to the weary and hungry Confederates pressing forward from Petersburg and Richmond in the vain hope of escape from the Federal troops, who were straining every nerve to overtake them and compel a surrender. To-night the cavalry corps was in their front and squarely across the road to Lynchburg, and it was reasonably certain, should our infantry get up in time on the morrow, that the almost ceaseless marching and fighting of the last ten days were to attain their legitimate result in the capitulation of General Lee's army.

As I stood there in the dark thinking over the work of the twelve preceding days, it was borne in upon me with startling emphasis that to-morrow's sun would rise big with the fate of the Southern Confederacy.

Just before daylight on the morning of the 9th of April, I sat down to a cup of coffee, but had hardly begun to drink it when I heard the ominous sound of a scattering skirmish fire, apparently in the direction of Appomattox Court-house. Hastily swallowing what remained of the coffee, I reported to General Sheridan, who directed me to go to the front at once. Springing into the saddle, I galloped up the road, my heart being greatly lightened by a glimpse of two or three infantrymen standing near a camp-fire close by the depot—convincing proof that our hoped-for reinforcements were within supporting distance.

It was barely daylight as I sped along, but before I reached the cavalry brigade of Colonel C. H. Smith that held the main road between Appomattox Court-house and Lynchburg, a distance of about two miles northeast from Appomattox Depot, the enemy had advanced to the attack, and the battle had opened. When ordered into position late the preceding night, Colonel Smith had felt his way in the dark as closely as possible to Appomattox Court-house, and at or near midnight had halted on a ridge, on which he had thrown up a breastwork of rails. This he occupied by dismounting his brigade, and also with a section of horse-artillery, at the same time protecting both his flanks by a small mounted force. As the enemy advanced to the attack in the dim light of early dawn he could not see the led horses of our cavalry, which had been sent well to the rear, and was evidently at a loss to determine what was in his front. The result was that after the first attack he fell back to get his artillery in position, and to form a strong assaulting column against what must have seemed to him a line of infantry. This was most fortunate for us, for by the time he again advanced in full force, and compelled the dismounted cavalry to slowly fall back by weight of numbers, our infantry was hurrying forward from Appomattox Depot (which place it had reached at four o'clock in the morning), and we had gained many precious minutes. At this time most of our cavalry was fighting dismounted, stubbornly retiring. But the Confederates at last realized that there was nothing but a brigade of dismounted cavalry and a few batteries of horse-artillery in their immediate front, and pushed forward grimly and determinedly, driving the dismounted troopers slowly ahead of them.

I had gone to the left of the road, and was in a piece of woods with some of our cavalrymen (who by this time had been ordered to fall back to their horses and give place to our infantry, which was then coming up), when a couple of rounds of canister tore through the branches just over my head. Riding back to the edge of the woods in the direction from which the shots came, I found myself within long pistol range of a section of a battery of light artillery. It was in position near a country road that came out of another piece of woods about two hundred yards in its rear, and was pouring a rapid fire into the woods from which I had just emerged. As I sat on my horse quietly watching it from behind a rail fence, the lieutenant commanding the pieces saw me, and riding out for a hundred yards or more towards where I was, proceeded to cover me with his revolver. We fired together—a miss on both sides. The second shot was uncomfortably close, so far as I was concerned, but as I took deliberate aim for the third shot I became aware that in some way his pistol was disabled; for using both hands and all his strength I saw that he could not cock it. I had him covered, and had he turned I think I should have fired. He did nothing of the sort. Apparently accepting his fate, he laid his revolver across the pommel of his saddle, fronted me quietly and coolly, and looked me steadily in the face. The whole thing had been something in the nature of a duel, and I felt that to fire under the circumstances savored too much of murder. Besides, I knew that at a word from him the guns would have been trained on me where I sat. He, too, seemed to appreciate the fact that it was an individual fight, and manfully and gallantly forbore to call for aid; so lowering and uncocking my pistol, I replaced it in my holster, and shook my fist at him, which action he cordially reciprocated, and then turning away, I rode back into the woods.

About this time the enemy's artillery ceased firing, and I again rode rapidly to the edge of the woods, just in time to see the guns limber up and retire down the wood road from which they had come. The lieutenant in command saw me and stopped. We simultaneously uncovered, waved our hats to each other, and bowed. I have always thought he was one of the bravest men I ever faced.

I rode back again, passing through our infantry line, intending to go to the left and find the cavalry, which I knew would be on the flank somewhere. Suddenly I became conscious that firing had ceased along the whole line.

I had not ridden more than a hundred yards when I heard some one calling my name. Turning, I saw one of the headquarters aides, who came galloping up, stating that he had been hunting for me for the last fifteen minutes, and that General Sheridan wished me to report to him at once. I followed him rapidly to the right on the wood-path in the direction from which he had come.

As soon as I could get abreast of him I asked if he knew what the General wanted me for.

Turning in his saddle, with his eyes fairly ablaze, he said, "Why, don't you know? A white flag."

All I could say was "Really?"

He answered by a nod; and then we leaned towards each other and shook hands; but nothing else was said.

A few moments more and we were out of the woods in the open fields. I saw the long line of battle of the Fifth Army Corps halted, the men standing at rest, the standards being held butt on earth, and the flags floating out languidly on the spring breeze. As we passed them I noticed that the officers had generally grouped themselves in front of the centre of their regiments, sword in hand, and were conversing in low tones. The men were leaning wearily on their rifles, in the position of parade rest. All were anxiously looking to the front, in the direction towards which the enemy's line had withdrawn, for the Confederates had fallen back into a little swale or valley beyond Appomattox Court-house, and were not then visible from this part of our line.

We soon came up to General Sheridan and his staff. They were dismounted, sitting on the grass by the side of a broad country road that led to the Court-house. This was about one or two hundred yards distant, and, as we afterwards found, consisted of the court-house, a small tavern, and eight or ten houses, all situated on this same road or street.

Conversation was carried on in a low tone, and I was told of the blunder of one of the Confederate regiments in firing on the General and staff after the flag of truce had been accepted. I also heard that General Lee was then up at the little village awaiting the arrival of General Grant, to whom he had sent a note, through General Sheridan, requesting a meeting to arrange terms of surrender. Colonel Newhall, of our headquarters staff, had been despatched in search of General Grant, and might be expected up at almost any moment.

It was, perhaps, something more than an hour and a half later, to the best of my recollection, that General Grant, accompanied by Colonel Newhall, and followed by his staff, came rapidly riding up to where we were standing by the side of the road, for we had all risen at his approach. When within a few yards of us he drew rein, and halted in front of General Sheridan, acknowledged our salute, and then, leaning slightly forward in his saddle, said, in his usual quiet tone, "Good-morning, Sheridan; how are you?"

"First-rate, thank you, General," was the reply. "How are you?"

General Grant nodded in return, and said, "Is General Lee up there?" indicating the court-house by a glance.

"Yes," was the response, "he's there." And then followed something about the Confederate army, but I did not clearly catch the import of the sentence.

"Very well, then," said General Grant. "Let's go up."

General Sheridan, together with a few selected officers of his staff, mounted, and joined General Grant and staff. Together they rode to Mr. McLean's house, a plain two-story brick residence in the village, to which General Lee had already repaired, and where he was known to be awaiting General Grant's arrival. Dismounting at the gate, the whole party crossed the yard, and the senior officers present went up on to the porch which protected the front of the house. It extended nearly across the entire house and was railed in, except where five or six steps led up the centre opposite the front door, which was flanked by two small wooden benches, placed close against the house on either side of the entrance. The door opened into a hall that ran the entire length of the house, and on either side of it was a single room with a window in each end of it, and two doors, one at the front and one at the rear of each of the rooms, opening on the hall. The room to the left, as you entered, was the parlor, and it was in this room that General Lee was awaiting General Grant's arrival.

As General Grant stepped on to the porch he was met by Colonel Babcock, of his staff, who had in the morning been sent forward with a message to General Lee. He had found him resting at the side of the road, and had accompanied him to Mr. McLean's house.

General Grant went into the house accompanied by General Rawlins, his chief of staff; General Seth Williams, his adjutant-general; General Rufus

Ingalls, his quartermaster-general; and his two aides, General Horace Porter and Lieutenant-Colonel Babcock. After a little time General Sheridan; General M. R. Morgan, General Grant's chief commissary; Lieutenant-Colonel Ely Parker, his military secretary; Lieutenant-Colonel T. S. Bowers, one of his assistant adjutants-general; and Captains Robert T. Lincoln and Adam Badeau, aides-de-camp, went into the house at General Grant's express invitation, sent out, I believe, through Colonel Babcock, who came to the hall-door for the purpose, and they were, I was afterwards told, formally presented to General Lee. After a lapse of a few more minutes quite a number of these officers, including General Sheridan, came out into the hall and on to the porch, leaving General Grant and General Lee, Generals Rawlins, Ingalls, Seth Williams, and Porter, and Lieutenant-Colonels Babcock, Ely Parker, and Bowers, together with Colonel Marshall, of General Lee's staff, in the room, while the terms of the surrender were finally agreed upon and formally signed. These were the only officers, therefore, who were actually present at the official surrender of the Army of Northern Virginia.

After quite a length of time Colonel Babcock came to the door again, opened it, and glanced out. As he did so he placed his forage-cap on one finger, twirled it around, and nodded to us all, as much as to say, "It's all settled," and said something in a low tone to General Sheridan. Then they, accompanied by General E. O. C. Ord, the commanding general of the Army of the James, who had just ridden up to the house, entered the house together, the hall-door being partly closed again after them, leaving quite a number of us staff-officers upon the porch.

While the conference between Generals Grant and Lee was still in progress, Generals Merritt and Custer, of the Cavalry Corps, and several of the infantry generals, together with the rest of General Sheridan's staff-officers, came into the yard, and some of them came up on the porch. Colonel Babcock came out once more, and General Merritt went back to the room with him at his request; but most, if not all, of the infantry generals left us and went back to their respective commands while the conference was still in progress and before it ended.

Just to the right of the house, as we faced it on entering, stood a soldierly looking orderly in a tattered gray uniform, holding three horses—one a fairly well-bred-looking gray, in good heart, though thin in flesh, which, from the accoutrements, I concluded, belonged to General Lee: the others, a thoroughbred bay and a fairly good brown, were undoubtedly those of the staff-officer who had accompanied General Lee, and of the orderly himself. He was evidently a sensible soldier, too, for as he held the bridles he baited the animals on the young grass, and they ate as though they needed all they had a chance to pick up.

I cannot say exactly how long the conference between Generals Grant and Lee lasted, but after quite a while, certainly more than two hours, I became aware from the movement of chairs within that it was about to break up. I had been sitting on the top step of the porch, writing in my field note-book, but I closed it at once, and stepping back on the porch leaned against the railing nearly opposite and to the left of the door, and expectantly waited. As I did so the inner door slowly opened, and General Lee stood before me. As he paused for a few seconds, framed in by the doorway, ere he slowly and deliberately stepped out upon the porch, I took my first and last look at the great Confederate chieftain. This is what I saw: A finely formed man, apparently about sixty years of age, well above the average height, with a clear, ruddy complexion—just then suffused by a deep crimson flush, that rising from his neck overspread his face and even slightly tinged his broad forehead, which, bronzed where it had been exposed to the weather, was clear and beautifully white where it had been shielded by his hat—deep brown eyes, a firm but well-shaped Roman nose, abundant gray hair, silky and fine in texture, with a full gray beard and mustache, neatly trimmed and not over-long, but which, nevertheless, almost completely concealed his mouth. A splendid uniform of Confederate gray cloth, that had evidently seen but little service, was closely buttoned about him, and fitted him to perfection. An exquisitely mounted sword, attached to a gold-embroidered Russia-leather belt, trailed loosely on the floor at his side, and in his right hand he carried a broad-brimmed, soft, gray felt hat, encircled by a golden cord, while in his left he held a pair of buckskin gauntlets. Booted and spurred, still vigorous and erect, he stood bareheaded, looking out of the open doorway, sad-faced and weary: a soldier and a gentleman, bearing himself in defeat with an all-unconscious dignity that sat well upon him.

The moment the open door revealed the Confederate commander, each officer present sprang to his feet, and as General Lee stepped out on to the porch, every hand was raised in military salute. Placing his hat on his head, he mechanically but courteously returned it, and slowly crossed the porch to the head of the steps leading down to the yard, meanwhile keeping his eyes intently fixed in the direction of the little valley over beyond the Court-house, in which his army lay. Here he paused, and slowly drew on his gauntlets, smiting his gloved hands into each other several times after doing so, evidently utterly oblivious of his surroundings. Then, apparently recalling his thoughts, he glanced deliberately right and left, and not seeing his horse, he called, in a hoarse, half-choked voice, "Orderly! Orderly!"

"Here, General, here," was the quick response. The alert young soldier was holding the General's horse near the side of the house. He had taken out the bit, slipped the bridle over the horse's neck, and the wiry gray was eagerly grazing on the fresh young grass about him.

Descending the steps, the General passed to the left of the house, and stood in front of his horse's head while he was being bridled. As the orderly was buckling the throat-latch, the General reached up and drew the forelock out from under the brow-band, parted and smoothed it, and then gently patted the gray charger's forehead in an absent-minded way, as one who loves horses, but whose thoughts are far away, might all unwittingly do. Then, as the orderly stepped aside, he caught up the bridle-reins in his left hand, and seizing the pommel of the saddle with the same hand, he caught up the slack of the reins in his right hand, and placing it on the cantle he put his foot in the stirrup, and swung himself slowly and wearily, but nevertheless firmly, into the saddle (the old dragoon mount), letting his right hand rest for an instant or two on the pommel as he settled into his seat, and as he did so there broke unguardedly from his lips a long, low, deep sigh, almost a groan in its intensity, while the flush on his neck and face seemed, if possible, to take on a little deeper hue.

Shortly after General Lee passed down the steps he was followed by an erect, slightly built, soldierly looking officer, in a neat but somewhat worn gray uniform, a man with an anxious and thoughtful face, wearing spectacles, who glanced neither to the right nor left, keeping his eyes straight before him. Notwithstanding this, I doubt if he missed anything within the range of his vision. This officer, I was afterwards told, was Colonel Marshall, one of the Confederate adjutants-general, the member of General Lee's staff whom he had selected to accompany him.

As soon as the Colonel had mounted, General Lee drew up his reins, and, with the Colonel riding on his left, and followed by the orderly, moved at a slow walk across the yard towards the gate.

Just as they started, General Grant came out of the house, crossed the porch, and passed down the steps into the yard. At this time he was nearly forty-two years of age, of middle height, not over-weighted with flesh, but, nevertheless, stockily and sturdily built, with light complexion, mild, gray-blue eyes, finely formed Grecian nose, an iron-willed mouth, brown hair, full brown beard with a tendency towards red rather than black, and in his manner and all his movements there was a strength of purpose, a personal poise, and a cool, quiet air of dignity, decision, and soldierly confidence that were very good to see. On this occasion he wore a plain blue army blouse, with shoulder-straps set with three silver stars equi-distant, designating his rank as Lieutenant-General commanding the armies of the United States; it was unbuttoned, showing a blue military vest, over which and under his blouse was buckled a belt, but he was without a sword. His trousers were dark blue and tucked into top-boots, which were without spurs, but heavily splashed with mud, for once he knew that General Lee was waiting for him at Appomattox Court-house, he had ridden rapidly across country, over road and field and through woods, to meet him. He wore a peculiar, stiff-brimmed, sugar-loaf-crowned, campaign hat of black felt, and his uniform was partly covered by a light-weight, dark blue, waterproof, semi-military cloak, with a full cape, unbuttoned and thrown back, showing the front of his uniform, for while the day had developed into warm, bright, and beautifully sunny weather, the early morning had been damp, slightly foggy, and presaged rain.

DEPARTURE OF GENERAL LEE AFTER THE SURRENDER

As he reached the foot of the steps and started across the yard to the fence, where, inside the gate, the orderlies were holding his horse and those of several of his staff-officers, General Lee, on his way to the gate, rode across his path. Stopping suddenly, General Grant looked up, and both generals simultaneously raised their hands in military salute. After General Lee had passed, General Grant crossed the yard and sprang lightly and quickly into his saddle. He was riding his splendid bay horse Cincinnati, and it would have been difficult to find a firmer seat, a lighter hand, or a better rider in either army.

As he was about to go out of the gate he halted, turned his horse, and rode at a walk towards the porch of the house, where, among others, stood

General Sheridan and myself. Stopping in front of the General, he said, "Sheridan, where will you make your headquarters to-night?"

"Here, or near here; right here in this yard, probably," was the reply.

"Very well, then; I'll know where to find you in case I wish to communicate. Good-day."

"Good-day, General," was the response, and with a military salute General Grant turned and rode away.

As he rode forward and halted at the porch to make this inquiry, I had my wished-for opportunity, but my eyes sought his face in vain for any indication of what was passing in his mind. Whatever may have been there, as Colonel Newhall has well written, "not a muscle of his face told tales on his thoughts"; and if he felt any elation, neither his voice, features, nor his eyes betrayed it. Once out of the gate, General Grant, followed by his staff, turned to the left and moved off at a rapid trot.

General Lee continued on his way towards his army at a walk, to be received by his devoted troops with cheers and tears, and to sit down and pen a farewell order that, to this day, no old soldier of the Army of Northern Virginia can read without moistening eyes and swelling throat.

General Grant, on his way to his field headquarters on this eventful Sunday evening, dismounted, sat quietly down by the road-side, and wrote a short and simple despatch, which a galloping aide bore at full speed to the nearest telegraph station. On its reception in the nation's capital this despatch was flashed over the wires to every hamlet in the country, causing every steeple in the North to rock to its foundation, and sending one tall, gaunt, sad-eyed, weary-hearted man in Washington to his knees, thanking God that he had lived to see the beginning of the end, and that he had at last been vouchsafed the assurance that he had led his people aright.

THE END

FOOTNOTE:

[1] This explanation is interesting because it represents a view more prevalent at that time than this. But the historians of to-day would not give the conflict over slavery as the first and chief cause of the Civil War.

[EDITOR.]

Milton Keynes UK
Ingram Content Group UK Ltd.
UKHW030911151124
451262UK00006B/827